*"Under the circ___
I don't think we ___
again."*

"Circumstances?" Her eyes were wide with unshed tears, but her chin was up and her back straight. "What circumstances, Linc?"

He reached across the table toward her, then withdrew his hand. "You're only going to be here for a little while, and it isn't fair to either of us to... You're a beautiful woman. You're warm and loving, and I—I could very easily..." He took a deep breath. "I could fall in love with you, and I don't think that's a good idea."

"Because of who I am," she said. "Or, rather, who I was."

He looked at her.

"Because you believe all the stories you've heard about me. Because it was so easy for you... I was easy, wasn't I, Linc? That's why you decided we shouldn't see each other again."

"I'm sorry," he said. "This isn't the way I wanted it to work out."

"All right, Linc." Eden stood up and started to turn away, but she hesitated, then shoved her plate of eggs Benedict across the table. In slow motion, it tilted and fell, upside down, onto Linc's lap. "Enjoy your breakfast."

Dear Reader,

With all due fanfare, this month Silhouette *Special Edition* is pleased to bring you *Dawn of Valor*, Lindsay McKenna's latest and long-awaited *LOVE AND GLORY* novel. We trust that the unique flavor of this landmark volume—the dramatic saga of cocky fly-boy Chase Trayhern and feisty army nurse Rachel McKenzie surviving love and enemy fire in the Korean War—will prove well worth your wait.

Joining Lindsay McKenna in this exceptional, action-packed month are five more sensational authors: Barbara Faith, with an evocative, emotional adoption story, *Echoes of Summer*; Natalie Bishop, with the delightful, damned-if-you-do, damned-if-you-don't (fall in love, that is) *Downright Dangerous*; Marie Ferrarella, with a fast-talking blonde and a sly, sexy cynic on a goofily glittering treasure hunt in *A Girl's Best Friend*; Lisa Jackson, with a steamy, provocative case of "mistaken" identity in *Mystery Man*; and Kayla Daniels, with a twisty, tantalizing tale of duplicity and desire in *Hot Prospect*.

All six novels are bona fide page-turners, featuring a compelling cast of characters in a marvelous array of adventures of the heart. We hope you'll agree that each and every one of them is a stimulating, sensitive edition worthy of the label *special*.

From all the authors and editors of Silhouette *Special Edition*,

Best wishes.

BARBARA FAITH
Echoes of Summer

Silhouette Special Edition

Published by Silhouette Books New York

America's Publisher of Contemporary Romance

To Kim Kelsey Strasburg
With love,
"Tia" Barbara

SILHOUETTE BOOKS
300 East 42nd St., New York, N.Y. 10017

ECHOES OF SUMMER

Copyright © 1991 by Barbara Faith

ISBN: 0-373-09650-X

First Silhouette Books printing February 1991

Printed in the U.S.A.

Books by Barbara Faith

Silhouette Intimate Moments

The Promise of Summer #16
Wind Whispers #47
Bedouin Bride #63
Awake to Splendor #101
Islands in Turquoise #124
Tomorrow is Forever #140
Sing Me a Lovesong #146
Desert Song #173
Kiss of the Dragon #193
Asking for Trouble #208
Beyond Forever #244
Flower of the Desert #262
In a Rebel's Arms #277
Capricorn Moon #306
Danger in Paradise #332
Lord of the Desert #361

Silhouette Special Edition

Return to Summer #335
Say Hello Again #436
Heather on the Hill #533
Choices of the Heart #615
Echoes of Summer #650

Silhouette Books

Silhouette Summer Sizzlers 1988
"Fiesta!"

BARBARA FAITH

is a true romantic who believes that love is a rare and precious gift. She has an endless fascination with the attraction a man and woman from different cultures and backgrounds have for each other. She considers herself a good example of such an attraction because she has been happily married for twenty years to an ex-matador she met when she lived in Mexico.

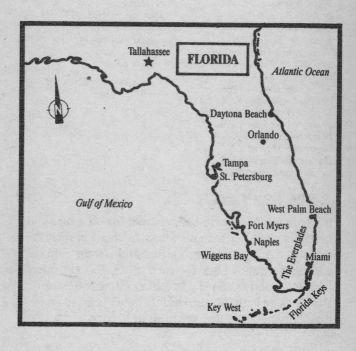

Prologue

She hadn't known it would be like this, hadn't known her body would break in two.

"Please," she whispered. "Oh, please, make it stop."

"You've got to push," he said.

"I can't."

"You have to."

She looked at the face half covered by the green mask. All she could see were his cinnamon eyes, angry eyes.

She wished he was Dr. Castillo. Dr. Castillo wouldn't let her suffer like this.

"You've got to help me," he said. "Come on, Eden, push."

"So tired."

"Push, dammit!"

A pain unlike any other pain tore through her body. She cried out with it, rode with it, and hung on until he said, "Yes, Eden. That's it. Your baby's here, Eden."

She lay back, weak and spent, arms and legs trembling from the terrible effort, so tired she didn't ever want to move. Then she heard the baby's cry, her baby. "What . . . what is it?" she asked.

"A girl," he said. "You have a little girl."

"Let me see her."

"You can't, dear," a nurse said.

"Let me hold her."

"That's against the rules, Eden."

"Please," she begged. "Just once. Just for a minute."

"I'm sorry." The nurse who was holding the baby turned away.

"Give her to me," the doctor said.

"We're not supposed to—"

He laid the baby on Eden's breast. She looked at the tiny red face, she felt the warmth of the child's body, and kissed the little scrunched-up face. "Don't cry," she whispered. "Everything's going to be all right."

He lifted the child off her breast and handed it to the nurse.

"Please." Eden raised herself on her elbows. "Oh, please," she whispered. "Don't take her away."

But it was too late. The nurse went quickly through the door, and it swung closed behind her.

It had been a long day and Linc McAllister was tired. He checked his patients on the second floor. Old Mr. Turner could go home tomorrow, he'd told the nurse. But they'd better keep an eye on Mrs. Beard. Check her every fifteen or twenty minutes, he'd cautioned. Call him if there was a change.

He went up to pediatrics, into the nursery. It smelled of baby lotion and talcum. He spoke briefly to the nurse in charge and looked at each of the three babies he'd delivered that day. A nurse sat in a rocking chair giving Eden Adair's baby a bottle. He hesitated a moment, then rested his hand on the child's head.

"It's late, Doctor," the nurse holding the baby, said.

Linc nodded. "I'm going to look in on the mothers before I go."

The corridor was quiet. There was only the soft pad of his rubber-soled shoes against the clean tile floor. He pushed open the door of Mrs. Alexander and Peg Tilton's room. Both women were asleep. He moved down to the room next door. His sandy brows came together in a frown and he hesitated a moment before he pushed it open.

Eden Adair lay on her side, her face turned into the pillow. Her small body shook with the force of sobs that came from somewhere deep down inside her, sobs of a grief and despair that were painful to hear.

He crossed the room and stood for a moment looking down at her before he sat on the edge of the bed. "Don't do this to yourself." He touched her shoulder. "You'll make yourself ill."

But she didn't stop and so, because he could not help himself, he put his arms around her and brought her up against his chest. She stiffened, then like a lost child she clung to him. He held her, his hand against the back of her head, her face against his shoulder. He felt her tears against his throat.

Finally, when she had wept all of her tears and all that remained were small, exhausted, sighing gasps, he laid her back against the pillows.

She looked up at him. Her face was swollen from crying. Her eyes, washed by her tears, were as green as the sea.

A sigh shuddered through Linc. He wanted to tell her that everything was going to be all right, that she was seventeen and she had her whole life ahead of her. In time she would forget.

But because he knew she would never forget he only said, "Try to rest now," and before she could speak, he turned and left the room.

Chapter One

The white clapboard house with the bright yellow door was three blocks from the beach. Crotons and red hibiscus grew like a hedge on one side of the yard. A big white oak covered most of the lawn, and purple bougainvillea grew halfway up one side of the house.

Eden turned off the air conditioner when she stopped the car, and leaning her head back against the seat she sniffed the warm air that drifted in a translucent humid haze over the lazy afternoon.

Little had changed in the years she'd been away. The town of Wiggins Bay was still the same sleepy, charming Florida town Eden remembered. The century-old banyan tree shaded the square and stately royal palms lined the street leading down to the beach.

It was good to be back, even though there was a sadness mixed with the memories of that long-ago summer.

She smiled, remembering the expression on her Aunt Jo's face when she'd stepped off the train in Miami that summer day so long ago. She'd been wearing a dark blue skirt and a white blouse, a navy blue cardigan and navy shoes with sensible heels, all selected by her father's new wife. Her pale blond hair had been pulled straight back from her face into a ponytail that hung down to the middle of her back, and there'd been an uncertain smile on her face because she hadn't been too keen on spending the summer in Florida with an aunt she barely knew.

Josephine DeWitt Taylor Hunnicut Browne, a thrice-married widow in her early forties, had been different from anyone Eden had ever known. She'd had bright red hair, "bottle red," she'd called it, long silver fingernails, a flair for wonderfully colorful clothes, an off-the-wall sense of humor and a salty vocabulary. She loved ice-cold beer, pretzels and peanuts, catfish and hush puppies, and she could stand for hours fishing off the end of the pier trading gibes and jokes with old-time Florida crackers.

The day after Eden arrived in Wiggins Bay, Aunt Jo had taken her shopping. She'd bought her jeans and shorts, T-shirts and sandals, summer dresses and bikinis. When Eden had protested that she really couldn't let her aunt buy so many expensive things, Aunt Jo had said, "I don't know who in the hell's been buying your clothes, kiddo, but whoever it was, has their taste in their mouth. You're young and you're beautiful, and at least while you're here you're not going to go around looking like somebody's maiden aunt."

Aunt Jo had brought laughter and warmth and love to a loveless child. Now she was dead and Eden would always grieve for her.

"She died in her sleep," Phoebe Rose had said when she phoned Eden. "The doctor said it was her heart. I should have suspected something. I should have—"

"It wasn't your fault," Eden had assured her. Phoebe Rose had been her aunt's housekeeper for almost thirty years. She'd cooked and cleaned and almost always sat in on Aunt Jo's weekly poker parties. She filled the house with Baptist hymns and a laugh that came from down deep inside. Eden knew how she must be grieving and she'd said, "I'll come on the next plane."

"There's no need for you to do that, chile. Miss Jo didn't want a funeral. A year or so ago she said, 'When I die, bury me and be done with it. And later, when Eden comes, the two of you call up some of my pals and hoist a couple of drinks.' So you just take your time, Miss Eden. I'll take care of things here."

The school term had had another week and a half to go, so Eden waited until the day after school ended and then she packed her car and set out for Florida. She was sorry she hadn't come back to Wiggins Bay before, but Aunt Jo had understood why she hadn't and she'd come often to Ann Arbor to visit Eden. They'd toured Europe together three years ago and last year they'd taken a Mediterranean cruise.

Her aunt had been delighted when Eden had told her she was coming to Wiggins Bay this summer. "It's time you returned," she'd said. "The past is past. Everyone's forgotten by now."

But she hadn't liked the reason for Eden's wanting to return. "It's wrong," she'd said. "Leave it alone."

But Eden wasn't going to leave it alone. She had almost three months to do what she'd come to do. Nothing was going to stop her.

Eden flexed her shoulders and got out of the car. She went around to the trunk, took her suitcases out, and started up the walk and onto the wide front porch. Before she could knock, the door opened and Phoebe Rose, wiping her hands on her apron, stood looking at her from behind the screen door. Then the door opened and Phoebe Rose put her arms around her.

Still as straight and spare as Eden remembered, her short hair had touches of gray now, but her fine dark skin was as unlined as it had been sixteen years ago.

"About time you got here," she said when she let Eden go. "I was in the kitchen and I didn't hear you drive up. Are you all right? I been worrying about you driving that long way all alone." She held Eden away from her and with a shake of her head said, "My, oh my, aren't you something else. Prettier'n even the first time I saw you. Now let's get you inside so you can rest. We'll be having dinner soon, but there's time to put your feet up and have a nice cool lemonade."

She helped Eden carry her bags into the house and once inside, insisted Eden "sit a spell." When she came back with the lemonade, she sat in a straight-back chair facing Eden. After Phoebe Rose had told her about her Aunt Jo's death and burial, she said, "You'll be wanting to call Mr. Prentice soon's you're settled in. He's got Miss Jo's will and he said to tell you things are fixed up so everything'll be real easy. I reckon that's because Miss Jo put the house in your name a few years back."

"I reckon so," Eden said, then smiled because she hadn't said 'reckon' in sixteen years. She'd picked the expression up from Phoebe Rose that long-ago summer and Aunt Jo had laughed and said, "Your daddy's going to have a fit if you keep saying that when you go back to Michigan."

* * *

But Eden hadn't gone back to Michigan. The way things had turned out she'd stayed with her aunt for almost a year.

The evening shadows lengthened and the hour grew late as she and Phoebe Rose talked about the woman they had both loved. They told funny stories about her, laughed a little, cried a little and finally they went into the dining room together and ate the dinner that Phoebe Rose had prepared.

Eden didn't mention the other reason she'd come back to Wiggins Bay until after they had cleared the table and Phoebe Rose brought in the Key lime pie.

"I want to see Dr. Castillo while I'm here," Eden said. "I'll call him tomorrow."

"Dr. Castillo died three months ago, Miss Eden, but Dr. Linc's still there. He's doing real well, too. I reckon half the folks in Wiggins Bay go to him. Your Aunt Jo liked him a lot and he took real good care of her. Days when she didn't feel up to going into his office he'd come by here to see her. He always said he'd come for some of my hush puppies but we both knew it was an excuse to check on her." Phoebe Rose's brows came together in a concerned frown. "What's the matter, Miss Eden? Are you ailing?"

"No, no, it's nothing like that," Eden said with a shake of her head. "I... I want to try to find out about the baby."

"The baby?" Phoebe Rose's dark eyes widened. "But you can't do that, Miss Eden. You gave the baby up. There're laws to protect the people who adopted her. You can't—"

"I just want to know for myself that she's well and happy and that the people who have her really care about her." Eden leaned forward in the chair. "I've thought about her for a long time Phoebe Rose, and I have to... I just have to know for myself that she's all right."

Then, because she didn't want to hear any of Phoebe Rose's arguments, she said, "I'm awfully tired. If you don't mind, I think I'll go up."

She stood and for a moment she rested her hand on the other woman's shoulder. "Don't worry about it," she said. "If I find her...when I find her I won't let her know who I am. I'd never do anything to cause her or the people who have her any pain." Her voice pleaded for understanding. "I just want to see her, Phoebe Rose. That's all. Just to see her."

The child she had given away.

Upstairs, in the room she'd had that long-ago summer, Eden decided she would start with Linc McAllister. He'd delivered her baby; he might know who the adopted parents were, and maybe if he understood how desperately she wanted to know about her child's welfare, he would help her. If he wouldn't, she'd ask Mr. Prentice to help her to open the court files.

She would do whatever she had to, but before she left Wiggins Bay she would see the child she had given up so long ago.

So long ago.

It had been a summer unlike any other. For the first time in her life she'd been free to wear pretty dresses and scanty swimsuits, to swim in the warm water of the Gulf of Mexico, to lie in the sun, to play and to make new friends.

She had spent every day at the beach, and on the second day there she'd met Marty Monroe. Marty, with her Florida tan, sun-bleached hair and bubbling personality, had taken Eden under her wing and had introduced her to everybody she knew.

There'd been picnics on the sand, volleyball, beach parties and dates. For the first time in her life Eden had felt pretty and popular—heady stuff for a girl who'd never been allowed to go to school dances or even to a movie with a boy.

Aunt Jo had opened her house to Eden's friends and Phoebe Rose had fried dozens of chickens and had made endless batches of potato salad and coleslaw. And though her aunt had encouraged Eden to date, she'd made sure that she met the young men first, that they called for Eden at the house and that Eden observed a midnight curfew.

The only young man that Aunt Jo had ever objected to had been Dave Fenwell.

"I distrust most high school jocks," Aunt Jo had said. "They all have broad shoulders, thick necks, and raging hormones."

But she hadn't forbidden Eden to go out with him.

To sixteen-year-old Eden he'd seemed like an all-American Adonis with his muscled, tan body and curly brown hair. She'd liked his kisses and his soft caresses and it had been exciting to be "Dave's girl." Sometimes his advances had frightened her though, and when he'd tried to French-kiss her, she'd pulled away and said, "Don't *do* that!"

"You'd better watch him," Marty had warned. "Dave's been around and I don't think you have."

And Shirley May Higgens, who'd dated Dave before Eden had arrived on the scene had said, "You think you're smart, but you just wait. As soon as Dave gets what he wants he'll drop you faster'n a gator can swallow."

Eden hadn't listened. Though she'd been frightened by all of the strange new feelings trembling through her body, she'd told herself that she wasn't a child and that she could handle Dave. Dave might have pushed and pleaded but she'd been sure that deep down he had respected her for being who she was.

There had been beer and wine at some of the parties, but Eden had always stuck to grape soda. And when her friends had kidded her about it, she'd said, "But I love grape soda. I'd drink it for breakfast if I could."

That's what she'd been drinking the night it had happened—grape soda that she hadn't known had been laced with vodka. Dave had his arm around her when they'd sat around the camp fire on the beach, and when he'd said, "C'mon, let's take a walk," she'd let him take her away from the others.

They'd walked barefoot along the shoreline. The water had been bathtub warm and the stars had looked close enough to touch. She'd looked up at them, wondering why that had made her dizzy, and she'd giggled when Dave had put his arms around her and kissed her.

"I'm dizzy," she said.

"Too much grape soda." He'd laughed, and then he'd kissed her again and when the kiss had ended he'd pulled her down on the sand with him.

"Listen," she'd said. "Maybe we'd better—"

He'd stopped her words with a kiss, and then they'd been lying side by side on the warm sand and he'd kept trying to pull her shorts down and she'd kept saying, "No, no, don't do that."

He'd rolled on top of her. He'd pinned her body with his legs. He'd got her shorts down and had pulled at her panties. She'd kept saying, "No, wait. Wait, please."

But Dave hadn't waited. He'd lunged against her, hurting and hard. He'd groaned and had said, "Oh, that's good! That's so good!" And when it had been over and he'd rolled away from her, he'd smirked and said, "Now don't that just beat all. Who'd have thought a girl as pretty as you would still have been a virgin?"

Eden hadn't gone back to the others. Instead she'd said, "I have to go home now." And though Dave had tried to make her go back to the party, she'd turned away from him and had hurried off into the darkness.

Dave had called her the next day but she wouldn't go out with him. She'd never gone out with him after that and a week later, Marty had told her he'd started dating Shirley May again.

When she'd stopped going to the beach, Aunt Jo had asked if she wasn't feeling well. Eden had answered that she had a school project she wanted to work on before the fall term started back in Michigan, and she'd begun spending her days at the library.

She had turned seventeen on August 10. By the end of the third week in August she'd known that she was pregnant, and because she was supposed to leave for Michigan the week after that, she'd finally told her aunt.

"I can't tell my father," she's said, stony faced with fear. "I'd die before I'd tell Dorothy."

Dorothy Hargreaves was the woman her father had married five months after Eden's mother's death. Every bit as straitlaced as Eden's father, Dorothy Hargreaves had restricted what few outside activities Eden had, and when Eden had brought home a B minus in algebra she'd grounded her for two weeks.

"Please," Eden had said, "please don't make me go back home."

Aunt Jo had taken her hand. "Have you told Dave?" she'd asked, and when Eden had said that she hadn't, Aunt Jo had told her that Dave had the right to know, and she'd called Dave and his parents and told them about Eden's pregnancy.

The three of them had come to the house. Aunt Jo had been pleasant; Eden had been silent. "We have a problem," Aunt Jo had said. "It doesn't only concern Eden, it concerns Dave, too."

"Doesn't have a damn thing to do with Davey," Frank Fenwell said. "We talked to him after you called and he admitted he and the girl had sex. But he wasn't the only one. She's been making out with half the boys in Wiggins Bay since the day you brung her here from Miami."

Aunt Jo's face had gone white, then almost as red as her hair, and Phoebe Rose had suddenly appeared in the doorway between the kitchen and the living room, one hand on her hip, the other clutching the meat cleaver.

Mamie Fenwell had said, "Really, Frank," and Dave had shuffled his feet and looked at his shoes.

"Davey has a football scholarship to the University of Miami this fall," Fenwell had said. "He sure hidey ain't going to ruin hisself by marrying this no-count niece of yours."

Aunt Jo ushered the three of them to the door. And after she'd closed it, she'd crossed to the sofa where Eden had been sitting and said, "I wouldn't let you marry that little son of a bitch if he was gold-plated all over." She'd taken Eden's hands in hers. "There are other options than marriage, honey. You can abort the child or you can stay here with me until it's born and put it up for adoption. If that's what you want to do, I'll call your father and tell him that I'm ill and ask him if you can spend the winter with me."

She'd put her arms around Eden. "It's going to be all right," she'd said. "I'll take care of you."

The next day Aunt Jo had called Eden's father. He'd said he'd discuss it with his wife, and an hour later he'd called back to say that Dorothy, good woman that she was, had agreed that Eden could spend the winter in Florida.

The following week Aunt Jo had taken Eden to see Dr. Castillo. Middle-aged, with graying hair and a pleasantly plump belly, he'd been kind and concerned and after those first few uncomfortable visits, Eden had begun to feel at ease with him.

But she'd never been at ease with his new young associate, Dr. Lincoln McAllister, because she'd sensed his disapproval from the moment she'd been introduced to him. He'd been twenty-seven, married and two years out of medical school. Twice when Dr. Castillo had been out on a case, Dr. McAllister had had to examine her. And though he'd been gentle, his manner had been only coolly polite, and she'd hated his touching her that way, seeing her that way.

The early morning that she'd gone into labor, Dr. Castillo had been in Nassau at a medical conference and Dr. McAllister had delivered her baby. He had stayed with her during those last painful hours and when she had begged, "Please, oh, please, don't let anything happen to my baby," he'd said, "Nothing will, Eden. I won't let anything happen to either one of you."

He'd brought her baby safely into the world and later he had come to her room and had held her while she'd cried. She hadn't seen him in sixteen years, but if he remembered her, and if he knew how badly she needed to know that the child she had borne was safe and well, perhaps he would tell her who had adopted her daughter.

Perhaps.

Chapter Two

The office had changed. There was a new nurse now, a receptionist and a bookkeeper. Yesterday the receptionist had asked if Eden had been a patient of Dr. McAllister's before.

"A long time ago," Eden had told her.

She stepped up to the receptionist's desk and said, "I'm Eden Adair. I have a two o'clock appointment with the doctor." And when the young woman had started to hand her a medical form to fill out Eden said, "I only want to talk to him."

"I see." A raised eyebrow indicated that the receptionist wondered why, but the question wasn't asked.

Eden picked up a magazine and leafed through it without really seeing anything. She thought about Dr. Castillo and about how kind he'd been to her and wished she were seeing him instead of young Dr. McAllister. A smile tugged at one corner of her mouth. That's how the patients had referred to him sixteen years ago; he wouldn't be that young now, he'd be in his early forties.

She wondered if she would recognize him, wondered if he would still have that look of quiet disapproval when he spoke to her. And she thought, yes, he'll disapprove when he finds out why I've come.

"The doctor will see you now."

The nurse waited by the door leading into the doctor's office and the examining rooms. Eden hesitated for the briefest of moments because all of the fear, the shame and the humiliation she'd felt so long ago came back and it was all she could do not to pick up her purse and head for the outer door. But she didn't, of course. She'd have faced the devil himself if it meant finding her daughter.

Dr. Linc McAllister didn't look anything like a devil. She'd remembered him as a serious, almost dour young man whose body hadn't quite caught up to his six foot, two inch height. But everything had come together and now he looked more like a forty-three-year-old line-backer than a doctor. His hair was still the sandy brown she remembered and his eyes really were the color of cinnamon.

He got up from behind his desk and reached across it to shake hands with her. Motioning her to a chair he said, "Miss Adair?" in a deeply resonant voice. "Have we met?"

"It was a long time ago, Dr. McAllister. I was really a patient of Dr. Castillo's but you..." This was harder than she'd thought it would be and she had to clear her throat and start again. "But you delivered my baby."

"That must have been soon after I came in with Dr. Castillo," he said with a smile.

"Yes, I believe it was. My first name is Eden, Doctor. Josephine Browne was my aunt."

"Eden." The sandy brows came together. "Eden Adair?"

Linc stared at the woman across the desk from him. And as though it had been yesterday, he suddenly and clearly remembered the frightened teenager whose baby he had delivered so many years ago.

Her aunt had called Dr. Castillo when the girl had gone into labor, but he had taken the call and he'd been waiting at the hospital when she was brought in. She'd been upset when she'd learned that he would deliver her baby, but afterward she had been brave and good and when the pains had been bad and she'd cried out, she'd said, "Sorry...sorry," as though she'd felt it necessary to apologize for hurting.

The poised young woman in the dark green sleeveless dress who sat across from him bore only a faint resemblance to the girl she had been. Her hair had darkened to a rich honeyed blond and the long ponytail had been replaced by a stylish shoulder-length cut. But the green eyes were the same, and it seemed to him that her mouth was as vulnerable now as it had been so long ago.

"I remember you," he said.

"I was so sorry to hear about Dr. Castillo."

A shadow of pain crossed Linc's face. "It was a heart attack. He died before we could get him to the hospital." He straightened the papers on his desk. "I'm sorry about your aunt. I'd been treating her for the last two years. She was a remarkable woman."

"Yes, she was."

"I suppose you've come back to settle her estate. How long will you be here?"

"I'm not sure. I have the summer off from school." And when she saw the question in his eyes she said, "I'm a teacher. I don't have to be back in Ann Arbor until the middle of September."

"Did you want to ask me about your aunt's illness? Is that why you came to see me?"

Eden shook her head. "No, I..." She tightened her hands around the white purse. "No, I wanted to see you because you delivered my baby."

The hand that had been straightening his papers stilled.

"I want to find her. I want..." She took a shaky breath. "I need to know where she is, that she's all right."

His face went cold and still. "Adoption records are sealed by law," he said.

"But laws change." Eden leaned forward in her chair. "Carter Prentice is handling Aunt Jo's affairs. I'm going to talk to him about trying to get the file opened."

"That's impossible. They won't do it."

"If the court refuses, I'll hire a private detective," she went on as though she hadn't heard. "There must be some way—"

Linc shoved his chair back and stood up. "You gave your child away a long time ago, Miss Adair. You can't suddenly decide that you want to see her, that you want to play at being a mother, to make trouble for everyone. Don't you know how upsetting it would be to a child to suddenly discover a mother she didn't even know existed? Have you any idea how it might affect her life? The lives of the people who adopted her?"

"That's not what I..." Eden clutched the edge of the desk. "I wouldn't do that. I only want to know that she's all right, that she's well and happy and cared for. I'd never hurt her or the people who've cared for her all these years." She felt her control beginning to slip. "She's my daughter," she whispered. "I have the right—"

"Whatever right you had, you gave up sixteen years ago," Linc said.

They stared at each other across the wide mahogany desk. Tears rose but did not fall from Eden's eyes. She stood up and in as calm a voice as she could manage, she said, "Thank you for your time, Dr. McAllister. I won't bother you again."

She reached the door before he said, "Miss Adair...Eden?"

She hesitated with her hand on the knob and looked back at him.

"Leave it alone."

She took a shaking breath. "I can't," she said. Before he could say anything more, she went out and closed the door behind her.

That Saturday night Eden gave a party for some of her aunt's friends. Most of them were the men and women Jo had played poker with every Friday night, and some were her fishing buddies, old men who, like Aunt Jo, could stand all night at the end of the pier, fishing pole in their hands, telling tall tales of better days and bigger fish.

Clyde Taylor, one of Aunt Jo's former husbands, drove in from Decatur, Georgia, and two ex-beaux came, one from Key West and the other from Ocala.

Marty Monroe, now Marty Collins, was the only one from the younger crowd Eden had kept in touch with over the years and Eden was pleased when Marty had said she'd love to come to the party.

There was plenty of cold beer on tap, and bourbon for the more hearty drinkers. Phoebe Rose had spent the day in the kitchen, and the dining room table was filled with plates of fried chicken, hush puppies, potato salad, bean salad, several different kinds of cheese and cold cuts, biscuits, corn fritters and sweet potato pie.

There were stories to tell, most of them funny ones about Aunt Jo. As the night wore on, one of the old men who had brought a guitar began to play, and after that, Phoebe Rose sat down at the baby grand piano in the living room and sang some of the old songs in her rich, full voice. Later on, the ones who were still left gathered around the table for another piece of pie and a last cup of coffee before they headed home.

"It's been a mighty fine evening," they said when Eden walked them to the door. "Your aunt would'a been pleased. This was just the kind of a party she liked. You'all want anything, you just let us know."

When Eden went back into the dining room, Marty, her long legs stretched out in front of her, said, "That was a good party, Eden. It was nice of you to give it."

"Phoebe Rose said that's what Aunt Jo wanted."

Marty shoved her chair back. "Come on, let's get this mess cleared up."

"We'll do it in the morning."

"From the sounds in the kitchen, I'd say Phoebe Rose is doing it right now."

"But I told her not to." Eden started into the kitchen with Marty one step behind. "Out," she said to Phoebe Rose.

"I'm just straightening up."

"No, you're not." Eden took the towel out of the other woman's hands. "You've been in the kitchen all day. It's my turn now."

And though Phoebe Rose argued that this was her job, Eden steered her toward the door. "It's been a long day," she said. "Go to bed."

And at last, complaining about folks getting too big for their britches, Phoebe Rose tromped off to her room.

"This reminds me of the parties we used to have here," Marty said as she took the dishes Eden had rinsed and put them into the dishwasher.

"Me, too." She smiled at Marty. "I'm sorry your husband couldn't come. I wanted to meet him."

"He'll be back from Gainesville sometime tomorrow night. Our anniversary's next Wednesday and we're having a small dinner party at the yacht club. You're invited."

"Thanks, Marty, but I don't think—"

"No buts, Eden. You can't spend the summer cooped up in the house."

"I don't think I'm up to the yacht club. There are a few people I'd just rather not run into. People like the Fenwells."

"They won't be there. Mamie died a couple of years ago. Frank married again and moved to Pensacola." She put the last plate in the dishwasher. "Dave and Shirley May don't belong to the club."

"What's he doing now? I know he had a football scholarship to the University of Miami, but Aunt Jo never spoke about him in her letters and I never asked."

Marty laughed. "Old Dave lasted three months in Miami, then he came back here and went to work in his dad's filling station. He's still there. He and Shirley May got married right after he came back. They've got three kids now."

"Good for Shirley May."

"Better her than you, kiddo." Marty took her apron off and hung it on the back of the kitchen door. "I'd better get home, Eden, but I'll see you on Wednesday. Okay?"

"I don't know, Marty. I—"

"No buts, Eden. Charlie and I will pick you up a little before seven." She clasped Eden's hands in hers. "It's going to be all right," she said. "I absolutely guarantee you're going to have a good time."

Eden really hadn't wanted to go, but as she dressed for Marty's anniversary party that Wednesday night she found herself humming to the music on the FM station she was listening to. She dabbed musk-scented perfume in a few strategic places, and put on the two piece ivory linen dress with the hand-embroidered, hand-crocheted lace. She called it her dressing up demurely dress, and with it she wore ivory satin pumps, a pearl bracelet and earrings.

Phoebe Rose smiled when Eden came downstairs, "My, my," she said. "You look just like one of those rich ladies in the society pages of the *Miami Herald*." Then her eyes filled and she said, "And wouldn't your Aunt Jo love to see you in that dress." She got her handkerchief out of her apron pocket and wiped her eyes. "I shouldn't be doing this, not when you're all ready for a fine evening. But Lord, I do miss her, Miss Eden."

Eden put her arms around Phoebe Rose. "I know you do. You were her best friend. She couldn't have managed all these years without you."

She heard a car pull into the driveway and stop. Eden hugged Phoebe Rose and when she let her go she said, "Are you okay?"

Phoebe Rose dabbed at her eyes. "'Course I am. You go along and have a good time."

"I will," Eden promised. Then she squeezed the other woman's hand and turned to hurry out the door.

Charlie Collins was every bit as nice as Eden had hoped he would be. An inch or two shorter than Marty's five-foot-eight, he had a squarish build, laugh lines around his eyes, and one of the nicest smiles Eden had ever seen.

"There are only going to be eight of us tonight," Marty told Eden when they turned into the driveway leading to the club. "I invited Linc McAllister to make it an even number. His wife died a little over a year ago and since then, everybody's been after Linc to be their extra man."

Marty looked back at Eden. "Did you know Carolyn? She was Carolyn Dillon before she married. She was almost ten years older than we were so you probably didn't."

"No." Eden shook her head. "I don't think I did."

"All of Linc's friends have been trying to get him to go out more but he doesn't accept too many invitations. He's a special friend of ours though and he knows I wouldn't foist just anybody on him."

Linc McAllister was supposed to be her dinner partner? Eden clasped her hands together and tried to quell the urge to leap out of the car. After their conversation in the office he was the last person she wanted to see, and she knew he certainly wouldn't have any burning desire to spend the evening with her.

"Does he know that I'm supposed to be his date?" she asked carefully.

Marty shook her head. "I only told him that you were an old friend of mine and that I knew he'd enjoy meeting you. Or maybe you already know him. Yes, wait a minute. Of course you know him. He was working with Dr. Castillo when you . . ." Marty's face flushed. "Oh hell, Eden. I'm sorry. I didn't stop to think. Maybe you don't want any reminders of the past."

"No, it's . . . it's all right, Marty. I really don't mind."

But she did mind and it was all she could do to walk into the dining room of the yacht club, purposely a few steps behind Marty and Charlie.

Dr. McAllister was already at the table chatting with the two other couples who would make up the party of eight when he saw them come in. He stood up to grasp Charlie's hand and kissing Marty's cheek said, "Happy anniversary, you two." Then his face stiffened and he took Eden's hand and said, "Hello, Miss Adair. I didn't know you were a friend of Marty's."

"We met when I first came to Wiggins Bay," Eden said. "We've stayed in touch and a couple of years ago we spent a week together in New York."

She tried not to let her chagrin show when Marty introduced the other couples, friends of hers and Charlie's from Naples. Lincoln McAllister held out the chair next to him for her and when she sat down, the man on her other side poured champagne into her glass.

Toasts were drunk to Marty and Charlie and when the orchestra began to play "The Anniversary Waltz," Charlie took Marty's hand and led her onto the dance floor.

"He seems like a very nice man," Eden murmured.

"He is." Linc looked at her curiously. Dressed with understated elegant simplicity, she was such a perfect picture of a lady that it was difficult for him to equate this new image with the frightened, unsure-of-herself girl he remembered.

She said something to the woman across the table from her and when she did, her honeyed hair drifted against the line of her cheek and he caught the faint scent of her perfume. Another couple got up to dance and almost without thinking Linc asked, "Would you like to dance?"

Eden turned to look at him and because he saw the hesitation in her eyes he pushed his chair back, stood up and led her onto the dance floor.

"The Anniversary Waltz" segued into "Our Love Is Here To Stay." Her body was stiff against his and he knew that she was as uneasy with the situation as he was.

"I hadn't expected to see you tonight," he said.

"Nor I you. I'm sorry if I've ruined your evening, Dr. McAllister."

"Linc, and you haven't. I'm sorry if I was abrupt the other afternoon but I was surprised to see you, after so many years, I mean. When you said you'd come back with the idea of finding your daughter, I'm afraid I overreacted."

Eden kept her eyes level with the shoulder of his dark blue suit.

"It's something I think we should talk about, Eden. Maybe later, or if you'd like we could have lunch together tomorrow."

She raised her face to look at him and suddenly Linc became aware of her softness and her scents, aware of the press of her breasts against his chest, the line of her hip against his. He became aware of her as a woman, a beautifully sensuous woman.

Her green eyes, the color of the Gulf on a sunny day, looked into his. His chest constricted and his body tightened because he hadn't felt this way in years, certainly not for at least three or four years before Carolyn's death.

During those last few years she'd been so high-strung and nervous that most of the time he'd felt as though he were walking a tightrope, balancing himself between the fluctuations of her depression and her days of almost maniac excitement. The few times in those years when she'd let him come close he'd made careful love to her. But he'd always been afraid of how she would react.

In the year since her death he hadn't been with another woman, partly out of a sense of loyalty to Carolyn and partly because he hadn't met anyone he was attracted to. But holding Eden Adair this way, he felt an almost-forgotten warmth spreading through his body. To take his mind off of it he said, "Tell me about yourself, Miss Adair... Eden. You mentioned the other day that you're a teacher."

"Special education," she said.

"Married?"

"No." She shook her head and he felt the brush of her hair against his cheek. "I married in college. We were both too young. It only lasted a year."

"Children?" He hadn't wanted to ask but he couldn't stop himself.

"No." She looked up at him again. He saw the barely perceptible tremble of her full lower lip and wished he hadn't asked.

When the set finished they went back to the table. Through all of the champagne toasts and the dinner that followed, Linc continued to be intensely aware of her. It was obvious from comments Marty made that Eden had gotten her life together. She had returned to Michigan after the baby's birth and entered the University of Michigan. She'd worked all the time she was in school and through the master's program that earned her a degree in special education.

"I wish I'd finished college," Marty said. "But I married Charlie in my freshman year at Florida State. We spent our honeymoon in Ft. Lauderdale during spring break and I got pregnant. We thought maybe I'd go back to school after the baby was born but I got pregnant again and that was the end of my college days." She smiled ruefully. "I envy you your career, Eden."

"And I envy you your children," Eden said.

She was quiet after that, and though she smiled when someone spoke to her she didn't really take part in the conversation. She danced with Charlie and with one of the other men, and raised her glass each time one of the guests offered a toast to the anniversary couple.

A little after eleven Linc looked at his watch and said, "This has been great but I've got a busy day tomorrow. I'd better be getting home." He turned to Eden. "How about you? Can I take you home or would you like to stay a while longer?"

"Well, I—"

"We're going on to a club in Ft. Myers," Marty said before Eden could continue. "You're welcome to come with us of course, but it's liable to be a late night."

Eden hesitated. "If you don't mind," she said to Linc. "If it wouldn't be out of your way."

"Of course it won't be out of my way." He took her arm and when they had said their good-nights he led her out of the club.

"Have you seen the new marina?" he asked as they started toward the car.

Eden shook her head. "When I was here, there were only a few boats tied up to the wharf. There must be hundreds in the slips now."

"There are. One of them is mine."

"You've got a boat? What kind?"

"Forty-two foot motor sailer." He grinned. "Every man has to have a vice. The boat's mine." He hesitated. "You'll have to have a look at her sometime."

"I'd like that."

"Want to take a walk out on the pier?"

Eden nodded. The night was warm, and except for the whiff of a breeze that came in off the water, still and heavy with humidity. She had almost forgotten the climate here on this west coast of Florida, but as they walked out toward the end of the pier and she heard the gentle lapping of the water against the wooden piles she knew how much she had missed it.

Pelicans slumbered at the end of the pier, cormorants swooped low over the water looking for fish, and by the light of the moon, frigate birds, as graceful as airborne swans, hovered as though suspended over the calm Gulf waters.

A few fishermen, old men mostly, leaned with their elbows on the railing and stared out at the endless dark water. Now and then one of them turned to another and said, "Ain't bitin' tonight. Reckon it's the heat."

"Reckon so" the reply came.

But none of them made as though to leave.

"There's a part of me that's always missed Florida," Eden said. "It's good to be back."

There was a sadness in her voice, a longing for summer days and for a time in her life when things had been simpler. The moonlight touched her hair and Linc found himself wanting to put his hands through it, to lift the errant strands that the breeze had blown across her eyes and brush them back. He wished that she were not so pretty, so feminine and somehow so vulnerable. He wished that things were different.

And because he knew that if they didn't leave soon he would have to touch her, he said, "It's late. I have to be at the hospital early in the morning."

Eden turned away from the railing and with a sigh she said, "I'm not much of a fisherman but I'm a little like

Aunt Jo, I guess. I could stand here forever just watching the water. I—''

"I got somethin'," one of the old men cried, and with a whoop began to reel in his line.

"What is it?"

"Danged if I know. Can't see..." He pulled the line up toward the dock. "Oh hell damn," he said, "It's one of them birds. Went after my live bait. Lord, I hate that."

He pulled his line up over the pier. The bird, hooked by the mouth, flopped helplessly against the wooden boards.

"Oh, poor thing." Eden started toward the bird but Linc put a restraining hand on her arm.

"Maybe I can help," he said to the fisherman who stood over the bird.

It was a cormorant with almost a thirty-inch wing span. Linc reached down, and kneeling beside the bird he closed his hand over the wings to stop the terrible flapping. "Easy," he murmured. "Easy now." To the fisherman he said, "Hand me your pliers," and when the man did, Linc fastened them around the hook, twisted and pulled the hook free. Then, still holding the wings close to the struggling body, he raised up and with his arms outstretched he launched the bird out over the water.

It hung suspended for a moment, then it spread its wings and flew.

Linc watched, and conscious of Eden beside him he said, "He'll be all right now." He handed the pliers to the old fisherman before he turned back to her. Her lips were parted in the first real smile he'd seen all evening. It was a smile that lighted up her face and because he couldn't help himself he reached out and gently touched her cheek.

She didn't move; she only looked at him, her smile a little uncertain now.

"I'd better get you home," he said in a voice that sounded rough to his ears. "It's getting late."

She took a step backward. "Yes," she said, a little breathlessly. "Yes, it's getting late."

They said good-night to the fishermen but after that, on the way back to his car, they were silent. When they drove up in front of her aunt's house, Linc got out of the car and came around to open her door and walk with her up the broad front steps.

At the top step Eden hesitated. "Night blooming jasmine," she said. "Isn't it lovely?"

"Lovely." But he wasn't looking at the jasmine, he was looking at her. "Good night," he said, and then he kissed her.

He had meant it to be a light kiss, a good-night kiss. But that's not what it turned out to be. Her lips were warm and yielding and unbelievably soft. Her mouth trembled uncertainly against his but she didn't pull away.

He tightened his hands on her shoulders, and though he wanted, more than he'd ever wanted anything in his life, to pull her into his arms and hold her and kiss her until they were both weak with longing, he made himself let her go.

"We mentioned lunch tomorrow," he said. "Would one o'clock be all right?"

"Yes." She took a deep breath. "I have an appointment at eleven. One o'clock would be fine."

"Do you remember where the Sea Shanty is?"

Eden nodded.

"Then I'll see you there." He wanted to kiss her again but he knew if he did, he might not let her go. "Good night," he said, and before Eden could answer he ran down the steps to his car.

She stood there until the car disappeared around the corner. She touched the lips that were still warm from his kiss, and with a half-smothered sigh she turned and went into the house.

Chapter Three

Carter Prentice, a handsome balding man in his early sixties, looked at Eden from across his desk. "It isn't impossible," he said slowly, "but it is extremely difficult. The few cases I've known where the court agreed to open an adoption file were in cases where some kind of a medical necessity was involved, where the party seeking to open the file, usually the adoptive daughter or son, needed to find a biological parent because of a rare blood disease or something of that nature. Otherwise..." Prentice steepled his long thin fingers. "Otherwise I doubt that the court would agree to open the file."

"But you'll try?"

Prentice hesitated. "If you're quite sure it's what you want. The court is very protective, and rightfully so, of both the adopted child and the adoptive parents. It wouldn't only be the child who is involved, whose life could be affected if you chose to make it known you were the biological mother. The parents who've cared for the child all these years would be affected, as well."

Eden shifted nervously in her chair. "It's not my intention to disrupt anyone's life, Mr. Prentice. I simply want to know that my child is happy and cared for. I'm willing to pay whatever you ask—"

"It isn't a matter of money, ma'am. It's a matter of ethics."

Eden's back stiffened.

"If you'd been coerced into giving up your baby or if you hadn't known what you were signing it might be different. I mean if you'd been younger..." Prentice raised his eyebrows in question. "You were what? Sixteen, seventeen?"

"I was seventeen."

"Was it your decision to give the child up or did your aunt force you to do it?"

"It was my decision. My aunt suggested it but I went along with her decision because there wasn't any way I could have taken care of a child. My father wouldn't have helped me, and I couldn't have asked my aunt to take care of me." Eden looked down at her hands. "I didn't have any choice, I had to put her up for adoption."

"I understand that, Miss Adair, and if you want me to try to have the file opened, I will."

"That's what I want."

He nodded, then turning to a file that lay open on his desk he said, "Your aunt's will is all in order. She left money to several of her friends here in Wiggins Bay, and the amount of forty thousand dollars to her housekeeper, Miss Phoebe Rose Blanchard. The rest of it—the house, some mighty good stock and the money is yours. It'll be a few weeks before all the papers are filed and cleared."

"That's all right, Mr. Prentice. I'd planned on spending the summer in Wiggins Bay." Eden rose. "You'll let me know, about the adoption file I mean?"

"Yes, Miss Adair, I'll let you know." He got to his feet. "You said before that your purpose in finding your daughter is simply to make sure that she's all right. But I'm wondering if you're going to feel differently once you find her. If maybe you won't be able to help yourself from telling her who you are." His gray eyes were troubled. "It could do a girl a lot of harm to suddenly have her real mother turn up."

"She won't find out, Mr. Prentice." Eden picked up her purse. "You'll let me know what's happening?"

"Yes, of course. And I'll phone you when the papers for Miss Jo's will are ready." He went with her to the door. "You're going to be pretty well-off when everything's sorted out, what with the house and all. Have you ever thought about staying here instead of going back north?"

Eden shook her head. "I like Florida, Mr. Prentice, but I don't belong here. When the summer's over I'll go back home to Michigan."

To the apartment near the University of Michigan campus, Eden thought when she stepped from the air-conditioned building out onto the street. To her work and her small circle of her friends. To a busyness of days and of solitary nights that were broken by an occasional outing with a friend or an even more occasional date.

The word date made her glance at her watch to see how much time she had before her luncheon appointment with Linc McAllister.

She'd been uncomfortable with him at the party last night because she'd known that he didn't approve of her or of her main reason for coming to Wiggins Bay. When they'd walked out on the dock, some of her feelings of discomfort had ebbed, and when he'd taken the hook from the cormorant's mouth and launched the bird into the air she'd felt a warmth and a strange kind of kinship with him and with the bird that flew up into the darkness of the night.

Linc had suggested they have lunch today to talk about her wanting to find her daughter, and she felt a growing sense of unease about meeting him because it had been painfully clear that day in his office that he didn't approve. She didn't think he liked her very much and she wasn't sure why he had kissed her last night. Nor did she know why she had kissed him back, or why she'd felt so strangely bereft when he'd let her go.

Eden brushed her hair back from her neck and wished she'd worn it up, wished that she could look cool and poised today when she met him. But with the temperature in the high nineties, cool was certainly out of the question.

The air hung hot and heavy over the town square that looked much the same as it had sixteen years ago. The royal poinciana trees were a mass of orange-red flowers, and the fronds of the tall coconut palms swayed like large green fans in the barely perceptible noonday breeze.

Eden glanced at her watch. It was only a five-block walk down to the beach and the Sea Shanty restaurant, but she hadn't been out in the sun in a long time and she could feel her face starting to burn. She hesitated when she started past Miss Burly's Ladies' Boutique, then went in and bought a wide-brimmed straw hat in the same pale yellow shade as her dress.

"You're prettier'n a daffodil," Miss Burly said when Eden paid her. "Yaw'l have a fine day, hear?"

And feeling cheerier than she had since she'd left her lawyer's office, Eden replied, "You have a fine day too, Miss Burly," and went out onto the hot street, down toward the beach where Linc McAllister waited.

He saw her when she was a block away, and in spite of the tension at the thought of meeting her, he smiled. She looked like summer, like the old Sinatra song about golden summer days. She was heart-stoppingly beautiful.

"Am I late?" she asked breathlessly when she reached him.

"You're right on time." He wanted to put his finger under her chin and kiss her, right here on this sunlit street for half the people in Wiggins Bay to see. But because he couldn't, or wouldn't, he said, "Let's get inside where it's cool."

He had reserved a window table and once inside they followed the waiter through the restaurant to a table overlooking the Gulf.

"I like your hat," he said when she took it off and placed it on the chair next to her. "But your nose and cheeks are sunburned."

"I'd forgotten how hot the sun is when I started out this morning. I bought it when I left Mr. Prentice's office."

Linc frowned.

"I had to see him about Aunt Jo's will."

He waited.

"And . . . and about the adoption." She picked up the menu and pretended to read it so that she wouldn't have to see the sudden flare of anger in his eyes.

For a few moments Linc didn't say anything. He looked at the menu without seeing it and finally said, "How about stone crabs to begin with?"

They spoke little during lunch. Linc asked her about her work and the problems of the children in the school where she taught, and why she had chosen that particular kind of teaching.

"There are so many bright kids who don't have the opportunity to excel because very often public school teachers don't have the time to give handicapped kids special attention," she explained. "My classes are usually small so I can devote time to students with extra needs."

. Linc watched her face as she talked. She was obviously sincere about liking what she did and he felt a sense of relief, as well as a strange sense of loss because he knew that when the summer ended she would go back north to her job.

The stone crabs were cold and fresh, the mustard sauce just hot enough. The green salad was crisp and the red snapper was tasty. He waited until they had eaten and the table had been cleared before he said, "I'd like to talk about your opening the adoption files, Eden." He forced a smile. "I'm afraid I was surprised the other day in the office. I didn't mean to be unkind."

"That's all right," Eden said with a flutter of nervousness. "I understand that it must have been a surprise, my walking into your office like that. I thought that because you'd delivered my baby you might know who had adopted her. But I realize now that it wouldn't be ethical for you to tell me."

"No, it wouldn't be."

"If you knew, I mean."

His mouth tightened.

"Do you know?"

He started to speak just as the waitress brought their coffee.

"Dessert?" the waitress asked. "We've got fresh peach pie today."

"No thank you." Eden looked down at her plate and waited until the waitress moved on to another table. "I'm sorry," she said then. "I shouldn't have asked that. It's just that I want this so badly, so..." She looked across the table at Linc. "I held her once, for less than a minute before she was taken away from me. When the nurse carried her out that door she took a part of me away. I've never felt whole, Linc. There's always been a part of me that's missing."

"Eden—"

"No, let me finish." She took a deep, shaking breath. "I've awakened at night because I thought I could hear her voice calling for me, and I've lain in a cold sweat thinking that maybe she was in some kind of trouble, that maybe someone was mistreating her. Every time I heard of a child abuse case or..." She put her fingers over her lips as though to still their trembling and when at last she could go on she said, "I just want to know... I *have* to know that she's all right. That somebody loves her."

She turned away, but not before Linc saw the tears. He looked out at the calm blue water and watched a flutter of sea gulls swoop down over a shrimp boat before he said, "Adoption agencies are careful about placing children in good homes. They—"

"The way they were in New York when that little girl was put in a good home and later murdered?" Clasping her hands together, Eden leaned across the table. "She could be anywhere, Linc. In Ft. Myers or Naples, maybe even here in Wiggins Bay. I could pass her on the street and not even know she was my daughter. If you know who adopted her. If you—"

He reached across the table and covered her hand with his. "Leave it alone, Eden," he said.

"I can't."

"The court will never agree to opening the file. You won't find her, you—"

"I have to find her. I need to know. I—"

"*You* have to find her. *You* need to know. Think about her, Eden, and about the family who adopted her. You can't come back after sixteen years and decide you want to play mommy. For whatever reason, you gave up all rights to your child a long time ago. It's too late now, let it go."

"I can't let it go. I need—"

"What about her needs? Think how it would affect her if you suddenly walked back into her life?"

Eden's face was as pale as the white linen napkin she held to her lips. "I told you," she whispered, "I'd never do anything to hurt her. I wouldn't tell her."

"You say that now, but if you found her, if you saw her, it would be different."

"It wouldn't be. I swear it wouldn't."

Linc pushed his coffee cup away. "I have to get back to the office," he said. "Are you ready to leave?"

"No, I... No, I think I'll have another cup of coffee."

"Very well." He put some money on the table, then stood and looked down at her. "What you want to do is wrong," he said. "It could hurt a family, it could hurt you."

She looked up at him and he almost gasped aloud at the pain he saw in her wide green eyes before she looked away from him and bowed her head. He wanted to rest his hand against the soft gold of her hair, to comfort her and tell her that everything was going to be all right.

Instead he turned away and hurried out of the restaurant.

When she returned to the house that afternoon, Phoebe Rose said, "Miss Marty called. Wanted you to call her back." She looked up from the roast she was preparing for that night's dinner. "You look all done in. Is anything wrong?"

"No. Maybe I've had too much sun. I'm not used to the heat."

"Would you like a glass of nice cold tea?"

"I don't think so, Phoebe Rose. I think I'll just lie down for a little while. I'll call Marty from upstairs."

Eden felt oddly defeated, certainly deflated, as she climbed the stairs to her room. She hadn't really expected that Linc might help her, but she'd hoped, after last night, that he might understand her need to know that her daughter was well and happy. But he didn't understand.

She tried to tell herself that it didn't matter what Linc McAllister thought about her. She'd come to Wiggins Bay to settle up her aunt's affairs and to find her daughter. That's all that was important; when she'd accomplished what she'd come for, she'd leave.

She dialed Marty's number and when her friend answered she said, "Hi. Phoebe Rose told me you'd called."

"Two things," Marty said. "I wanted to know if you got home safely last night, what you thought of Linc, whether or not he made a pass, whether you accepted his pass and to find out if you'd like to play tennis tomorrow."

"That's more than two. Yes, I got home safely, and maybe I'd like to play tennis."

Marty laughed. "Hmm," she mused. "So what about Linc?"

"What about him?"

"Did he make a pass?"

"Don't be silly."

"Listen, having Linc McAllister make a pass isn't silly. Half the women in this town would jump at the chance of making it with a guy like Linc."

"I'm from Michigan," Eden said. "We're not as hot-blooded as you Florida crackers."

"Maybe you just need a little thawing out." Marty gave an exaggerated sigh. "I reckon this means you're not going to tell me whether or not you got kissed good-night."

"I reckon it does."

"Then how about tennis and lunch?"

"I haven't played for a couple of years, Marty."

"That's okay. We're playing for exercise, not for blood. I'll arrange for you to have a guest pass while you're here, and I'll pick you up at ten-thirty tomorrow. Okay?"

"Okay."

A little of Eden's tension had eased by the time she put the phone down. She'd always enjoyed playing tennis but she'd never been good at it. She'd see how it went tomorrow and if she wasn't too rusty maybe she'd take some lessons while she was here. It would do her good to get out of the house because if she didn't, all she'd do is sit around and wait for Mr. Prentice to call.

Yes, she'd be better off being active so that she wouldn't have to worry about whether or not Prentice would be successful in opening the court files. Or about how Linc McAllister's eyes turned from cinnamon to a hot, hard brown when he was angry.

Two young women were playing when Eden and Marty arrived at the club. Eden watched, marveling at how quickly they moved, how good they were, and she laughed at the friendly gibes they shouted at each other.

Both of the girls were tanned and pretty and it was fun to sit in the shade and watch them. The points were tied when one of them, a leggy blonde, lobbed a shot that dropped just over the net. The other girl tried for it but missed.

"Yahoo!" the blonde shouted, and as Eden and Marty watched, she dropped her racket and did a wild and whooping war dance around it.

"That's Kim McAllister," Marty said with a laugh. "Linc's daughter. She's a darling girl." She winked at Eden. "Almost as cute as her father."

The girls walked off the court. "All yours," said the one who had lost.

"Thanks, Elaine." Marty smiled at her, then at the leggy blond girl. "Hi, Kim," she said. "Great game."

"Thanks, Mrs. Monroe. The last point was pure luck. Elaine's really a great player." She looked at Eden and smiled.

"This is Eden Adair, Kim," Marty said. "She's an old friend and she's spending the summer here at Wiggins Bay."

"How come you picked summer?" Kim sat down on the grass near them and wiped her face with the blue scarf she'd had tied around her neck. "It's awfully hot, isn't it?" She looked up at Eden. "I love your name. It's really classy."

"Thank you," Eden said with a laugh. "I like yours, too." She hadn't known that Linc had a daughter. The girl, as Marty had said, was a darling. Tanned and pretty, with sun-blond hair, pale green eyes and a pleasantly wide mouth, she fairly bloomed with goodwill and good health.

"Have you played tennis here before?" Kim asked.

Eden shook her head. "As a matter of fact I haven't played tennis in a couple of years and I wasn't very good then, so Marty'll probably kill me."

"I could give you some pointers if you'd like. I mean I could watch you play and tell you what I think is wrong."

"That'd be great. You're a wonderful player."

"Thanks. I try to play every day in the summer. Sometimes on weekends I play with my dad. He's really great." She squinted up through the sun. "Do you know him?"

"I met him a long time ago. The other night Marty invited me to her anniversary party. Your dad was there, too."

"So it was like a date, right?"

"Not exactly," Eden said.

Elaine looked down at Kim. Whacking her thigh with her racket she said, "I'm gonna take a shower and head on home, Kim. Maybe Mrs. Monroe can give you a ride when you're ready to go."

"I'll be glad to," Marty said.

"Okay." Kim waved her hand at Elaine. "See ya."

"Yeah, see ya."

The game that followed was all one-sided. Eden got off a few shots, but the heat and the fact that she hadn't played for a while did her in and after one set she called it quits.

Kim had commented little during the game except to say, "Get farther back" or, "Watch it now, she's hitting to your right." But when Eden and Marty came off the court she said, "You're not too bad. I mean you sorta know what you should do. You just need a little practice. Your backhand is pretty limp and your serve is weak. If you'd like, I could maybe help you."

"I don't think I could even lift the racket right now."

"How about tomorrow morning? We could play a couple of sets and I could like tell you some of the things you're doing wrong."

"I'd like that fine," Eden said. "You're far too good to play with me but I could certainly use some help."

"We could meet at eight-thirty. It's not too warm then."

"Okay." Eden sat up. "You may end up throwing your racket at me but I'll do my best." She pushed her damp hair back off her face and got to her feet. "Marty and I are going to have lunch. Will you join us?"

"Sure. Thanks a lot. I'd like to."

Kim chattered all the way back to the clubhouse. How long had Eden known her dad? she wanted to know. Had her dad and Eden danced together at the anniversary party?

"He's okay at slow dancing," she said, "but he thinks the lambada is awful and he's never even heard of INXS." She grinned at Eden. "I bet you have."

Eden grinned back. "But only because I work with people your age and because I watch MTV just to see what's happening. I like some of Madonna's earlier songs, and I'm crazy about U2, but I can't stand heavy metal bands."

"Heavy metal bands. They're so killer! What about..."

The merits of popular music went on until they were seated at an outside table overlooking the marina. Eden and Kim both ordered lemonade and Marty asked for a gin and tonic and a basket of popcorn. "We can order lunch later," she said, "I have to cool off first." She smiled over at Kim. "What are you going to do this summer? Will you stay here in Wiggins Bay or are you and your dad going to take a trip somewhere?"

"We're talking about maybe a cruise to Mexico." Kim turned to Eden. "Have you ever been there?"

Eden nodded. "I went to Puerto Vallarta last year and I liked it a lot. A cruise sounds like fun."

"Maybe," Kim said, "but I think I'd just rather stay here for the summer."

Marty looked up when the waiter put their drinks and the basket of popcorn in front of them. "Thank God," she said, and took a sip of her gin and tonic. "I've never been so thirsty in my life. It must be over a hundred today."

"No, it's only about ninety-five." Kim reached for the pepper at the same time Eden did. "You, first," she said politely.

"Hey wait a minute." Marty looked horrified. "That's pepper. You want the salt."

"I like pepper on my popcorn." Eden sprinkled it on one section of the basket and handed the pepper shaker to Kim.

"So do I," Kim said with a laugh. "My dad thinks I'm totally weird. I even take a pepper shaker with me when we go to the movies and he's always saying, 'Don't put that damn stuff on my side of the box.'" She smiled across the table at Eden. "We're kindred spirits," she said.

When lunch was over Marty drove both Kim and Eden home. When she dropped Eden off, Eden said, "Thanks, Marty. I'm awfully glad you talked me into coming today. I had a lot of fun." She smiled at Kim. "I'll see you in the morning. Do you want me to pick you up?"

Kim shook her head. "No, my dad will take me there on his way to the office. But you can give me a lift home if that's okay."

"Sure. I'll be glad to. Maybe we'll have a late breakfast if you've got the time."

"Hey, that's great. They make yummy French toast—"

"Yeah, and the two of you will probably put pepper on it," Marty said.

Both Eden and Kim laughed. "See ya," Kim called out when Marty headed out of the driveway.

Eden watched them drive away. She was still smiling when she went into the house where Phoebe Rose said, "You look mighty happy, Miss Eden. I reckon you had a good time."

"I had a great time," Eden said.

Maybe it was going to be a pretty good summer after all, Eden thought as she headed upstairs for a shower. It would be fun playing tennis again, and fun to spend a little time with Kim McAllister. She was a nice girl, cute and lively and fun. She...

Eden paused with her hand on the banister. Linc hadn't mentioned that he had a daughter. Maybe he wouldn't like the idea of Kim playing tennis with her. He'd been angry when he'd left the restaurant yesterday. He didn't approve of her or of what she wanted to do, and she wasn't sure how he'd feel about her spending time with Kim.

Maybe Kim wouldn't tell him. Maybe she'd just say she was going to play tennis with some lady she'd met at the club. But if they played again...

Eden shook her head. She'd worry about that when the time came. In the meantime she was looking forward to seeing young Kim McAllister again.

Chapter Four

Linc lowered the morning paper. "Who did you say you played tennis with?"

"Eden Adair. I'm meeting her at the club this morning." Kim took a sip of orange juice. "That's why I'm not having breakfast now. We'll eat after the game."

Linc folded his newspaper and put it next to his plate. "I thought you usually played with Elaine."

"I'll play with her later."

"Where did you meet Miss Adair?"

"At the club. She was there yesterday with Mrs. Monroe. I watched the two of them play and then we had lunch together." Kim grinned. "Eden's really a terrible player. I said I'd help her today."

"I'm not sure I like the idea of your spending time with her, Kim. You and Miss Adair really don't have anything in common."

"Sure we do. We both put pepper on our popcorn." Kim laughed. "Would you believe it, Dad? We both reached for the pepper at the same time. I've never known anyone else who put pepper on popcorn. Awesome."

Linc's face tightened. "You should be spending time with friends who're your age, Kim. You can play tennis with her today because you've already made the date, but I'd rather you didn't do it again."

"But why?" Kim's chin came up. "I like her and I don't see any reason why I shouldn't play tennis with her if I want to."

Be careful, Linc warned himself. Be very careful how you handle this. He stood up and forcing a smile said, "We can talk about it later." Then, as though it were an afterthought, he said, "I'll stop by the travel agency today and pick up a couple of brochures. Some of the cruises go to the Caribbean and then Mexico."

"In a week?"

"No, it'd be closer to three weeks. I could take some time off. Do both of us good to get away for a while."

"I don't know, Daddy. I think maybe I'd just rather spend the summer here. Maybe we could sail down to the Keys or someplace." She stood on her tiptoes and kissed his cheek. "Gotta get my racket," she said. "Meet you at the car."

Linc stood where he was and watched her take the stairs two at a time. "Damn," he said softly. "Oh damn it all to hell."

Kim lobbed easy balls over the net and kept her criticisms to a minimum. She helped Eden work on her backhand and serve and after they'd played a set she said,

"You're doing okay. We'll play again tomorrow if you don't have anything else to do."

"I don't have anything to do," Eden answered when they headed toward the clubhouse, "but I don't want to take up too much of your time. I know I don't play a very good game so it can't be much fun for you. Wouldn't you rather play with your friend Elaine?"

"Elaine and I play later in the day. I like helping you." She smiled shyly up at Eden. "I like talking to you."

"And I like talking to you."

Eden tilted her face to the sun. It was a beautiful day, she'd played a fairly decent game of tennis and she enjoyed being with Kim.

When they were seated at a table overlooking the marina, they both ordered French toast with bacon. Eden said, "Really crisp, please."

Kim said, "Burn it," and they both laughed at the expression on the waiter's face.

"I hate soggy bacon," Kim said when he turned away.

"Or sausage that's undercooked."

"Dad does it exactly right. He always fixes breakfast on Sunday morning. Pancakes and sausage. He's been doing it for years, even when Mama was alive." Kim took a sip of her milk. "Did you know my mother?"

"No. I don't think so."

"She was really beautiful."

"Do you look like her?"

Kim shook her head. "No, I guess I look more like Dad. My mother had really pretty brown eyes and silky brown hair. Maybe mine will turn darker when I'm older." She reached for her bag, fumbled for her wallet, and when she found it she flipped through plastic-covered photographs and said, "This is my mother. Her name was Carolyn." She handed the wallet to Eden.

Eden studied the photograph. Carolyn McAllister had been a very beautiful woman, but her eyes were sad and her smile looked forced.

"She was sick a lot, I mean before she got pneumonia."

"You must miss her."

Kim nodded. "We didn't do a lot of things together because most of the time she wasn't feeling good, but I always knew she was there. I mean we could talk sometimes. You know?"

"I know. I lost my mother when I was just about your age."

Kim's eyes widened. "Then you really do know, don't you?"

Eden covered the girl's hand with her own. "Yes, I really do. It's like a part of yourself has been suddenly cut away from you and you don't understand why it has."

"Yes." Kim sighed. "I go up to her room sometimes. I read some of her books—she really loved poetry—and I just sit there like I'm waiting for her to come back." She hung her head and looked at Eden through lowered lashes. "I guess that sounds really dumb, doesn't it?"

"It doesn't sound dumb at all." She squeezed Kim's hand. "Is it okay if I look through the other pictures?"

"Sure." Some of the sadness went out of Kim's eyes and she leaned across the table so that she could tell Eden who everybody was. "That's Elaine," she said. "You met her yesterday. That's Becky and Karen. And Dad on his boat. He named it *Kimmer* after me. *Très* cool, don't you think?"

"*Très,*" Eden said with a smile. She'd never seen Linc in anything but a business suit or a white doctor's coat. He looked different in cutoffs and a T-shirt, tanned and fit, and leading man handsome.

"Here's one of the two of us together." Kim flipped to another photo. "Last summer after Mama died we sailed down to Cape Sable and Flamingo. Maybe this year we'll take the *Kimmer* down to the Keys. Dad wanted to take a cruise to the Caribbean and Mexico but I told him this morning that I didn't think I wanted to do that."

Eden took a sip of her coffee. "Did you mention that you were going to play tennis with me?"

"Uh...yes, I told him." Kim blushed and fiddled with her fork.

And he didn't like the idea, Eden thought with a sinking feeling. He doesn't want Kim spending time with me because of what happened when I was her age, because he thinks I might be a bad influence on her.

"That's Steve," Kim said, just as the waiter appeared with their breakfast.

Eden forced herself to focus on the photo that Kim had turned to. The boy looked a little older than Kim. He was tan and like Kim, his hair was bleached from being in the sun. "Cute," she said.

"Cute! He's super swass!"

"Swass?" Eden smiled. "What's that?"

"It's a guy who has everything. And believe me, Steve has everything." Her mouth drooped and she began to worry her lower lip with her teeth. "We broke up."

"I'm sorry, Kim. Did you have a fight?"

"Sort of." Kim looked around, then in a low voice she said, "He wanted me to...you know, do it with him."

Eden stared at her. Without thinking, she tightened her hand over the plastic-enclosed photograph.

"He said if I really cared about him I would."

"What did you say?"

"I told him no. I mean I couldn't. I want to wait until I'm older. You know? Like until I'm really sure I want to." Her eyes misted. "I like him so much, Eden, and when I said no he got really mad. Now he's going out with Megan Harper and I . . . I miss him a lot."

"Did you talk to your dad about this?"

"No!" Kim shook her head. "I could never do that. Daddy'd kill him. I told Elaine and she said that maybe I should try to get Steve back. She said that by the time you're sixteen..." Her face got red. "She said that we're not kids and that it was time we . . . you know." She looked imploringly at Eden. "What do you think? What would you do if you were me?"

Run for my life, Eden wanted to say. Instead she motioned for the waiter, and when he brought the check and she'd put some money on the table, she said, "Let's walk down by the marina. We can talk better there."

It would give her time to collect her thoughts, to find the words to try to help Linc's daughter. But she hardly knew Kim. Surely there was someone else, another woman Kim could talk to about this. But what if there wasn't? Kim's mother was dead and while it was obvious she had a good relationship with her father, it was also obvious she didn't feel comfortable talking to him about sex.

What she wanted to do was grab Kim by her shoulders and shout, Don't you dare even think about going to bed with that boy. You don't know what the consequences might be. You have your whole life ahead of you. Don't ruin it, don't take a chance of messing up your life the way I did.

Instead of going to the boat slips, they walked down the length of the old pier next to it. And when they'd taken off their shoes, they sat on the end of the pier and dangled their feet in the water. "Sex is kind of a scary subject," Eden said, "no matter how old you are. But I guess it's a lot more scary when you're a teenager."

Kim darted a look at her.

"It's such an important part of life, Kim, one of the most beautiful things that can happen between a man and a woman if it's right. If the two people really care about each other."

Eden stared out over the water. It hadn't ever been right with her. With Dave it had been little more than rape. With Artie it had been bearable but never enjoyable. That had probably been her fault. She'd been traumatized by her first abrupt encounter with sex, by the shame of her pregnancy and by having to give up her child. The failure of the marriage hadn't been Artie's fault; it had been hers.

Eden glanced at Kim's troubled face. I'm not the one to ask, she wanted to tell her, but because she was the one Kim *had* asked she said, "Okay, let's talk about this. In my opinion, Steve behaved selfishly and certainly immaturely when he tried to force you into a relationship you weren't ready for."

"Yes, but—"

"And when you wouldn't do what he asked he dropped you and started going with somebody else." Eden tried to keep the anger and indignation out of her voice. "That's not what a man does when he really cares about a woman, honey. It seems to me that Steve is a lot more concerned about himself than he is about you and your feelings."

"But I really miss him," Kim said in a voice so low Eden could barely hear her.

"I'm sure you do, Kim, and it isn't going to help to tell you that the world is full of wonderful young men who'd love to be going out with a girl as pretty and as nice as you are." She stroked the tangled blond hair back off Kim's face. "You're going to have zillions of boyfriends and lots and lots of happy times," she said. "One of these days you'll meet the right man, somebody who'll care about you and love you the way you should be loved. And when you do you'll know when the time is right for loving."

Kim's pale green eyes looked into Eden's. "Are you sure?" she whispered.

"I'm absolutely, positively positive." Eden smiled. "Okay?"

"Okay, and . . . and thanks for talking to me."

"This advice comes from my vast experience in never raising children of course," Eden joked.

"You should have children. You'd make a wonderful mother, Eden."

Something clutched at Eden's heart. "Maybe...maybe someday," she said. "And if I ever do, kiddo, I hope they're all exactly like you."

A manta ray swam near the pier and a school of flying fish zipped by. Eden and Kim sat in companionable silence, slapping the water with their feet, and at last, when the sun was high overhead, they picked up their tennis rackets and went back to Eden's car.

"Can we play tomorrow?" Kim asked when Eden dropped her off in front of her house.

"Yes, I'd like to."

Kim leaned one tanned arm on the door. "Maybe you could come over sometime when my dad's here, like for dinner or something."

"Maybe. Shall I pick you up in the morning or will your dad drop you off?"

"He'll drop me off." Kim stepped back from the car. "Eight-thirty," she said. "See ya."

Eden smiled. "See ya," she answered.

She and Kim played tennis the next three mornings. Eden's game improved and she finally stopped burning and started to tan.

It was the end of June now and the temperature was in the nineties almost every day, so after the tennis game they swam in the club's Olympic-size pool before they had breakfast. And though Eden loved spending time with Linc's daughter, being with Kim made her even more aware of how much she had missed not seeing her own daughter grow up.

Kim was a lovely girl—healthy, happy, and full of fun. She'd grown up with parents who loved her, and though Linc wasn't a wealthy man he was well enough off to provide all of life's necessities for his daughter. When the time came, Kim would go to a good college or university, and though her mother was dead, she would always know that her father was there for her.

Had her own daughter had any of the advantages Kim had had? Was she as healthy and happy as Kim? Would she go on to a college or a university?

These were the thoughts that troubled Eden when she was with Kim. What was her daughter doing? she wondered when she watched Kim streak across the tennis court or dive into the pool? Did she have the kind of life Kim had? Was her father as lovingly protective of her as Linc was of Kim?

A week had gone by since she'd seen Carter Prentice. He had said he would call if he had any information, but waiting was difficult.

Linc called on Saturday morning. The phone had been ringing when she came in from tennis, and Phoebe Rose said, "It's Dr. McAllister for you, Miss Eden."

She hadn't heard from him since they'd had lunch and when she took the phone from Phoebe Rose she felt a moment of nervousness.

"Hello," he said. "How's everything?"

"Just fine."

"I know this is kind of last minute, Eden, but I wonder if we could have dinner this evening."

"Dinner?" Her hand tightened around the phone.

"Would seven o'clock be all right?"

"Yes." She took a deep breath. "Yes, seven's fine."

"Good. I'll see you then. Goodbye, Eden."

"'Bye, Linc."

She put the phone down. "I'm going to have dinner with Dr. McAllister tonight."

"He's a mighty fine man. I reckon he's been lonesome since his wife died. Do him good to start dating."

Eden shook her head. "I don't think this is a date, Phoebe Rose. I think Dr. McAllister just wants to talk to me."

"About what?"

"Probably about his daughter. She's been helping me with my tennis and I have the feeling he doesn't like the idea of her spending so much time with me."

Phoebe Rose put her hands on her hips and frowned. "Now why wouldn't he want her spending time with you? The girl misses her mother and he ought to understand she needs to have somebody like you around."

"Somebody," Eden said bitterly. "But not me, Phoebe Rose."

"I'd like to know why not."

"Because of what happened a long time ago. I don't suppose he thinks I'm fit company for a girl like Kim." Eden started up the stairs to her room, but she paused midway and looked back at the other woman. "You were here the night the Fenwells came over with Dave. You heard what Mr. Fenwell said about . . . about my having had sex with half the boys in Wiggins Bay." She tightened her hand around the railing. "That probably wasn't the only time he said it, Phoebe Rose. I imagine he spread it all over town."

"Nobody would have believed him, Miss Eden, least of all somebody as nice as Dr. Linc." Phoebe Rose shook her head. "You shouldn't go thinking things like that. I reckon Dr. Linc's asking you out tonight just because you're pretty and nice and he wants to spend some time with you." She moved closer to the bottom step of the stairway. "The past is past, Miss Eden. It's time you forgot, time you got on with your life. I reckon having dinner with Dr. Linc is a mighty fine way to start." She winked at Eden. "I wouldn't be a'tall surprised but what you two don't get along just fine."

Chapter Five

"Have you been to Sanibel yet?" Linc asked when they started over the bridge to the island.

Eden shook her head. "I suppose it's changed a lot since I was here."

"New hotels," he answered with a nod. "But it's still one of the best places for shelling in the world."

"And for no..." Eden looked at him. "The sand fleas. I can't remember what you call them."

"No-see-ums," he said with a laugh. "And yes, they're still here."

He had asked her to have dinner with him tonight so that he could talk to her about Kim but Linc found that he was beginning to enjoy the evening. Eden was a remarkably pretty woman, but it was more than that. There was an air of honesty about her, a lack of pretense that he liked. Dressed as she was tonight in an off-the-shoulder white dress that went well with her newly ac-

quired tan, and with her hair back off her face in a
ponytail that she'd adorned with a gardenia, she looked
almost as young as she'd been the first time he'd seen her.

"There were only a couple of restaurants the last time
I was here," she said. "I remember one near the channel
between Sanibel and Captiva."

"That's where we're going. I was hoping we'd make it
before the sun went down but I'm afraid we won't."

When he left the bridge he pulled off the road and
clicked off the air-conditioning.

The sky was a blaze of red streaked with unbelievable
shades of orange, flamingo and gold. The waters of the
Gulf shimmered in iridescent splendor. Everything
stilled, as though the world, stunned by the beauty of the
moment, held its breath.

Out on the beach the shell seekers, some with their
heads down, others bent from the waist, searched for
prizes to take back to Ohio, New York, or Pennsyl-
vania—their gifts from the sea in remembrance of a
golden summer's day.

"It's so beautiful," Eden said softly. "I'd forgotten
how beautiful Florida sunsets can be."

In the reflection of the sun, her hair had turned to pure
gold, and her skin was like honeyed bronze. She looked
beautiful and vulnerable, and because he wanted to touch
her he tightened his hands on the steering wheel so that
he wouldn't.

Remember why you're here, he told himself as he
started the car. And he tried not to look at her until they
reached the restaurant.

The restaurant faced the Gulf. It was a pleasant place
with a breathtaking view of the beach. They spoke little
as they gazed out at the water and the darkening sky and
sipped cool white wine. Eden ordered a shrimp cocktail

with hot horseradish sauce, then pompano covered with slivered almonds.

"I'd almost forgotten that fish could taste this good," she said when she took the last bite of the pompano. "This was wonderful, Linc."

He nodded to the waiter as the red-jacketed young man removed their dishes and asked if they wanted coffee and dessert.

"Only coffee for me," Eden said.

When the waiter brought their coffee along with the check, Linc said, "How does it feel to be back in Florida after all these years? Don't you mind the heat?"

"Sometimes, but I try not to go out too much in the middle of the day."

"That's why you play tennis in the morning I suppose?"

"Yes." Eden took a sip of her coffee. "Kim's an awfully good player," she said carefully. "It's nice of her to help me but I've been worried about taking up so much of her time."

"Yes, so have I. She's missed a couple of all-day sailing parties with her friends just so the two of you could play tennis. I'm not sure that I like that."

"I didn't know she'd done that." Eden gazed out the window toward the beach to give herself a moment to think. "I know our being friends seems a little strange, Linc, especially because I'm so much older than Kim. But I feel such an affinity toward her, and I think she does toward me. Sometimes a girl Kim's age needs to talk to somebody who's older, to a woman I mean, because she lost her mother and—"

"She can talk to me," he said stiffly. "She's always known she could talk to me about anything."

"I'm sure she can, but I think it's easier to talk to someone outside the immediate family. That's the way I was with Aunt Jo. I could always tell her things I wouldn't have dreamed of telling my stepmother, or even my mother when she was still alive." Eden lifted her bare shoulders. "I'm a little like that with Kim. I—"

"Because of your vast experience in raising children?"

Eden's face went pale. For a moment she didn't answer and then in a quiet voice she said, "No, Linc, not because I've raised any children, but because I'm a woman and I was sixteen once."

"I remember."

She saw the coldness in his eyes, and with a sinking feeling she knew why he didn't want her to see Kim. He remembered that she'd been pregnant when she was Kim's age. He had heard and believed the stories that Dave and his father had told.

She took a deep breath to try to quell the sickness that threatened her stomach. All of the humiliation and the shame that had made her want to run away that long-ago summer made her want to run away now.

"No one ever really forgets, do they, Linc?" she said. "It doesn't matter who I am now or what I've made of my life. I'm still the same Eden Adair who got pregnant when she was sixteen."

"Damn it, Eden, I—"

"That's why you don't want me to see Kim, isn't it? You think that because of what happened I'm not the kind of person Kim should associate with."

"I didn't say that."

"Didn't you?"

He hated himself for doing this to her, for causing the look of sickness and shame on her face. He'd hurt her and that's not what he'd wanted to do, not what he'd meant to do.

"You believe the stories you heard," she went on. "The stories Mr. Fenwell told about Dave not being the only one that..." Her hands tightened into fists. "You believed them," she whispered.

Linc shook his head, but there was a moment's hesitation before he said, "No, I—"

She leaned across the table, her eyes level with his. "I was raped," she said. "Dave Fenwell threw me down on the sand and he raped me. He hurt me and there wasn't a damn thing I could do about it."

"Eden..."

She threw her napkin onto the table and pushed her chair back. Before he could stop her she turned and ran out of the restaurant.

Linc put some bills on the table and hurried to follow her. He called himself a jerk for what he'd said, for what he had to do. But he had to stop her from seeing Kim. They were getting too close; that scared the hell out of him.

He caught up with her just as she was leaving the parking lot headed for the road.

"Eden..." He put his hand on her arm but she shook it away. "I'm sorry," he said. "I didn't mean to hurt you."

"Go away."

"No, I won't go away." He took her hand and hung onto it. "Come on, you can't walk all the way back to Wiggins Bay." He led her back into the parking lot and when they reached his car he said, "Get in, Eden."

She shot him an angry look, hesitated, then got in. They drove all the way through Ft. Myers and Bonita without speaking, but when they got to Wiggins Bay he said, "Why don't we have a drink and talk about this?" Without giving Eden a chance to refuse he headed for the club.

When he parked the car he took her hand again and led her toward the sandy beach instead of to the bar.

The only light came from the last quarter of a fading moon. The only sound was the gentle lapping of water against the shore. She didn't want to be here with him. He'd hurt her. He didn't think she was the kind of a woman his daughter should associate with. He'd believed the stories Mr. Fenwell had told. He'd believed that she'd slept with all those other boys.

Pain ripped through her, deep and hot and shattering. Angry tears formed and because she didn't want Linc to see them she turned away, and taking off her sling-back pumps she waded into water still warm from the day's sun. Everything was quiet now, and in the distance she could see the lights of a passing freighter.

"Eden?"

Her shoulders stiffened. She looked back toward shore. Toward him.

He had taken his jacket off and he was standing, legs apart, his back to the lights from the club. His face in the shadows looked ruggedly handsome, and troubled.

She wished she could make him understand that she wasn't trying to take his wife's place in his daughter's affections, that all she was offering was friendship and understanding. And that in a way she couldn't explain Kim was giving her something, too. She was giving her a glimpse at what her own daughter might be like.

As suddenly as it had come her anger faded. She understood Linc's concern for Kim, she understood a little of how difficult it must be to raise a daughter alone.

The sand was warm under her feet when she came out of the water. She stood for a moment looking up at the sky, unaware that Linc had moved closer until he said, "I'm sorry that I hurt you, Eden. I know you were raped. I know the stories Dave Fenwell's father spread were lies."

He still remembered how he'd felt the day he'd learned the truth, and how it had taken every ounce of his willpower to keep his hands off young Fenwell.

Dr. Castillo had heard the stories that Dave and his father had circulated about Eden and he'd asked Dave to come into the office. He and Linc had faced him together.

Dave had lied at first, but Dr. Castillo had kept after him and finally Dave had told them the truth about how he'd spiked Eden's soft drink and taken her down the beach away from the others, and how he had forced himself on her.

"How was I to know she was a virgin?" Dave had said. "I thought she wanted it. I thought . . ."

He'd gone after Dave, ready to strike, when Dr. Castillo had grabbed his arms and held him back.

"Don't, Linc," Castillo had said. "He isn't worth it."

Now Linc smoothed the fair hair back off Eden's face and said, "I didn't mean to hurt you. I'm sorry."

Eden took a steadying breath. "You're being protective of Kim. I understand that, Linc. If she were my daughter I'd be protective, too."

He flinched as though from a physical blow and turned away, but not before she'd seen the look of shock and pain on his face. She touched his arm. "What is it?" she asked. "What—"

He shook his head, and because he could no longer help himself, he put his arms around her.

She felt the tension in his body and without thinking she drew him closer as though to comfort him.

They stayed like that for a long moment and when he let her go he said, "Maybe we'd better have that drink now."

She stepped away from him. "I'm really not much of a drinker. Do you think we can get coffee at the bar?"

"I doubt it but I know somebody who makes terrific coffee." A slight smile softened his features. "I've been wanting to show you my boat and this seems like a good time to do it."

He took her arm and she let him lead her down the beach to the marina and out onto the dock. The *Kimmer* was in the last slip. He stepped down to the boat, then reached up his hand to help Eden aboard.

"Come on below and let me show you around," he said. "I'll fix the coffee and we can take it back up on deck." He unlocked the cabin door and reached in to switch on a light before he took her hand and led her down into the cabin.

The galley, though small, was as well equipped as any modern kitchen. There was a microwave, a two-burner stove, and a small refrigerator. Beyond the galley there was a dining nook, a lounging area, and beyond that a cabin and a bathroom.

"Kim and I spend some of our weekends here," Linc said as he busied himself in the galley. "She's a great little sailor. We're talking about sailing down to the Keys sometime this summer."

"That'll be nice."

He wanted to ask her if she'd like to come with them, but because he knew that he shouldn't, and because he was curious about her life in Michigan, he said, "What about you? Do you do any sailing?"

Eden shook her head. "I haven't been on a boat in years."

"What do you do in the winter? Are you a skier?"

"Yes, but I'm not very good. Friends and I go at least once every year."

"Any special friends?" He measured coffee into a pot and added a stick of cinnamon. "A special friend?" he asked. "A man?"

Eden shook her head. "I don't date all that much."

"That's hard to believe."

She smiled uncertainly.

"Eden..." Linc hesitated. "Eden, I'm sorry if I hurt you tonight at dinner. I didn't mean to. And I certainly didn't mean to infer that because of what happened a long time ago I didn't think you were good enough for Kim. It isn't that. It..."

The roar of a speedboat almost drowned out his words. The *Kimmer*, caught in the wake, began to rock.

Eden stumbled and he reached out a hand to help her. "Damn speedboats don't pay any attention to the speed limit. They..."

She was close to him, her hand against his chest to steady herself. She looked up at him. No, he thought, I won't...

But suddenly she was in his arms and he was holding her so close he could feel her heart beating. He said her name and then he kissed her the way he'd been wanting to kiss her ever since he'd picked her up tonight.

Her lips were soft and warm against his and though she whispered, "No, we..." her arms crept up around the back of his neck.

It's just a kiss, he told himself. I'll let her go in a moment. All I have to do is step away.

But his arms, as though of their own volition, tightened around her. He put one hand against the back of her head to hold her closer. He felt the heat of her body and his own instant response.

Her lips parted under his. He touched the tip of her tongue and felt an answering response. The kiss deepened. Heat flooded through him. He had to stop.

He held her away and looked down at her. Her mouth was tremulous and her eyes were soft with desire. "Eden?" he whispered, and kissed her again.

She knew she should stop, but it was heaven to be held by him, to be kissed by him. She'd never known kisses like his, had never known the kind of warmth that kindled inside her, the kind of urgency when the warmth became a flame.

He cupped her breasts and she moaned aloud. He ran his thumbs across her pebble-hard nipples and instead of pushing him away she covered his hands with hers to hold him there. She couldn't think; there was a fever in her blood. She had to stop. Had to...

Linc eased the white dress lower so that he could kiss her bare shoulders. He trailed hot kisses over her throat, nibbled her ears and covered her mouth with his again.

Eden was lost in an ecstasy of feeling that was part agony, part pleasure. She wanted more. She pulled at the buttons of his shirt and opened it so that she could run her fingers through the thick matt of his curly chest hair.

He drew her closer and she felt the tickle of his hair on her breasts, and without conscious thought rubbed them against his chest.

Linc groaned deep in his throat and the sound sent a shock of pleasure through her.

"Yes," he said. "Oh yes." He cupped her breasts and held her away so that he could kiss them.

"Sweet," he whispered against her skin. "So sweet."

His mouth scalded her, his tongue and his teeth drove her toward a brink of feeling she'd never experienced before.

"Oh, please," she said, not sure whether she was pleading for him to stop or to never stop.

Her body began to tremble. Somewhere in the back of her mind where she could still think she knew that she had to stop while there was still time. She ran her fingers through his thick sandy hair to push him away from her, but instead her fingers tightened and she held him there while he caressed her with his mouth.

He let her go and gripping her shoulders he looked deep into her eyes. "Eden?" he said.

She touched the side of his face and trailed trembling fingers across his lips.

A tremor ran through Linc's body and with a sigh he took her hand and led her to the sofa in the lounge. He kissed her, his mouth warm and gentle against hers. "I want to undress you," he said.

"Linc...Linc, I..." She took a shaky breath, and not taking her gaze from his, she raised her arms so that he could pull the dress over her head.

Clad only in white satin panties she stood for a moment, arms at her sides, looking at him. "Now, you," she said.

He unfastened his belt and took his trousers off. Without taking his gaze from hers he hooked his thumbs under his briefs.

He was magnificent. She knew that she would never forget the way he looked standing here before her.

He put his arms around her. "You're so soft," he whispered against her hair. "So sweet."

He drew her to the sofa and when she lay down he slipped the white satin panties down over her hips and lay beside her.

She felt his hardness against her thigh.

"Wait." She stiffened with the old remembered fear. "No, wait. No, please. I . . ."

"What is it?" he asked. "Tell me, Eden."

"Nothing." Shame made her turn away. "I . . . I'm sorry."

Linc put his arms around her and held her close. "It's going to be all right," he said against her hair. "I won't hurt you, Eden. I won't do anything you don't want me to do." He kissed her trembling mouth, he caressed her breasts, and only when he felt in her the same urgency that raged through his body, only when she said, "Oh yes," did he grasp her hips and join his body to hers.

Eden turned her head into his shoulder, afraid if she didn't she would cry out with the sheer pleasure of having him inside her. He moved with exquisite slowness. He sought her mouth and kissed her deep and hard, and his hands went around her back to cup her bottom and rock her closer.

She clung to him. She hadn't known that anything could be this good, that she could be this *one,* this heart-breakingly close to another person, to move with him, be part of him.

Her body throbbed with pleasure. Her hips lifted to his and she moved as he moved. Small whispers of pleasure drifted in incoherent sound from her lips.

He said, "So good. Oh, Eden, oh, sweetheart, it's so good."

He began to move more fiercely, stroking more deeply. He plunged, he withdrew, and plunged again. The breath came fast in his throat and he said, "Eden? Eden?"

She tried to answer, tried to say his name, but there were no words to tell him. Her body was out of control. She tightened her hands around his shoulders and lifted herself to him as she cried out in a shattering ecstasy of feeling.

He thrust his body against hers and sought her mouth. "Oh yes," he whispered. "Oh yes."

And he held her close while his body tightened and shuddered over hers.

"I knew," he said. "I always knew it would be like this with you."

They took their coffee up on deck, and when they settled back into the chairs Linc reached for Eden's hand.

The water was calm. The club had closed and there was only one light flickering from the stanchions along the dock. A slight breeze came in off the Gulf and her hair, freed from the ponytail during their tumultuous love-making, drifted like a golden cloud about her face.

His body felt lighter, more relaxed; he couldn't remember ever having felt this sense of rightness, this sense of being so powerfully masculine that he wanted to beat his chest and shout with primitive, hedonistic joy.

He tried to tell himself all of the reasons why he and Eden shouldn't have made love, but his body was still too alive from her touch; he was still so very aware of her. He closed his eyes and it seemed to him he could still hear her sighs and whispers, her small murmurs of pleasure, that one final joyous cry of completion.

"It's late," she said.

He opened his eyes. "About what happened..." He hesitated. "I didn't plan it. I mean that's not why I brought you here."

"I didn't think you had."

She was such a confusion of emotions. Guilty, sad, worried that he would think she'd been too easy, that because she'd been this way with him she was like this with other men. She couldn't stand it if he thought that.

But stronger than her guilt and her sadness and her worry was an all-pervading sense of wonder, a marvelous feeling of . . . so *that's* the way it's supposed to be! *That's* how you're supposed to feel when it's right.

It had never been right for her before. She hadn't known, hadn't even imagined that anything could be so good. Good! What a little word for such an immensity of feeling! She felt as though her whole body had somehow been freed, that in that last shattering moment she changed from the person she had been to someone new and better and yes, triumphantly wiser.

She wanted to smile. She wanted to tell him. She wanted to say, I've never felt like this before. No one has ever made me feel what I felt with you.

But because she couldn't say any of those things she closed her fingers tightly around his hand.

A little while later Linc said, "It's late. I'd better take you home. I'll just go below and lock up."

He got up, but instead of leaving he put his hands on either side of her chair and leaning down he gently kissed her.

When he went into the cabin to get her purse and turn off the light he smoothed out the sofa cushions and straightened the pillows. When he touched one of them he saw the gardenia Eden had worn in her hair.

He picked it up. It was fragile and small in his hand. It would bruise so easily, as easily as Eden would bruise. He closed his eyes and rubbed it against his lips. Eden, he thought, and not knowing why he did, he opened his wallet and tucked the gardenia inside.

Chapter Six

"Dad said he had dinner with you last night."

"Uh, yes," Eden said. "We went to Sanibel."

"Did you have a good time?"

"Yes, we had a...a very nice time. The dinner was good. I...I've always loved Sanibel. The beach is so pretty there. I mean the shelling is wonderful. And the sunsets are..." Eden took a deep breath. "The sunset was fantastic last night."

Kim took a swing at the grass with her racket. "How did you and my dad get along?"

"We got along just fine, Kim." Eden hesitated, and not sure what Kim's reaction was to her having gone out with Linc, she said, "Do you mind that I went out with your dad?"

"Of course not." Kim looked surprised that she'd asked. "It's just that he doesn't really date. I mean he hasn't since Mama died."

"I'm not sure it was a date," Eden said carefully. "Your dad and I knew each other a long time ago. He was my aunt's doctor as well as her friend and I think that's the kind of friends we are."

"Gosh, I hope not!"

It was Eden's turn to be surprised. "You don't want your dad and me to be friends?"

"Sure, that's okay, but I'd like it a lot better if you were like...you know, like his girlfriend. Then the three of us could take trips together. We could take the boat down to the Keys and maybe around to some of the islands and—"

"Whoa." Eden smiled. "You're getting ahead of things here. Just because your dad and I had dinner doesn't mean we're dating."

"Don't you like him?"

"Of course I like him."

Kim grinned.

"I mean...your father's a very nice man. He—"

"And he's good-looking, too, don't you think?"

"Yes, he is, but..." Eden didn't know what to say. Although she was relieved that Kim wasn't upset because she'd had dinner with Linc, she was suddenly overwhelmed with feelings of guilt. She and Linc had made love and in a way she couldn't explain it seemed to her almost like a betrayal of her friendship with his daughter. And though she longed to see him again and was hurt that he hadn't suggested it, she didn't want Kim to get the idea that she and Linc were dating, that there was anything other than friendship in their relationship.

Forcing a smile she said, "Yes, I think your dad is good-looking. Now can we play tennis?"

"Okay." Kim gave an exaggerated sigh. "If you really don't want to tell me what happened last night." She bounced the tennis ball, then looking earnest, she said, "Dad's a pretty neat guy, Eden. For somebody his age, I mean. And he can do anything. He's a really great doctor. He can sail a boat and cook and he can fix things like sinks or just about anything that's broken. He's really terrific."

Eden wanted to hug Kim because Kim liked her enough to want there to be a romance between her father and her new friend. But she'd be leaving Wiggins Bay when summer ended and there really couldn't be anything between herself and Linc. And because Eden knew it was best not to get Kim's hopes up, not to think about something that couldn't happen, she trotted over to the other side of the net and called, "Let's go."

They played two sets and by the time they had finished the sun was hot and the temperature had climbed into the high nineties. When they came off the court and started up to the clubhouse, Eden wiped her face with her kerchief and heading for the shade of the palm trees, said, "Let's rest for a couple of minutes."

"Okay." Kim flopped down beside her and they lay back on the grass together.

"Do you ever make pictures out of clouds?" Kim asked.

Eden nodded, and pointing skyward she said, "There's an old man ... there ... see him? See his cap? His bushy eyebrows and his jutting nose? Those little puffs in front of him are sheep."

Kim squinched her eyes. "Uh-uh. It's a guy with an IRoc driving along a beach road." She was silent for a moment and then she said, "Steve's got an IRoc." She turned her head so that she could look at Eden. "He called me last night."

Eden rolled onto her side. "What did he say?"

"He asked me to go out with him."

Eden's brows came together in a frown. "What did you say?"

"I said I'd think about it." Kim plucked a blade of grass and began to flip it across her cheek. "I'd like to see him," she said.

"Kim..." Eden hesitated. Kim wasn't her daughter. Their relationship was rather a curious one because of the difference in their ages, but she had a feeling Kim wouldn't have mentioned Steve's calling if she hadn't wanted to talk about it.

"I suppose it wouldn't do any harm to talk to Steve," Eden said at last. "But unless he's changed in his thinking I don't think you should see him again."

"But I really like him." Kim rolled onto her stomach. "He's so cool, Eden. He's handsome and he's got great shoulders. He's probably going to get a football scholarship to the University of Miami when he graduates. He even dates older women, like college women. Elaine told me that he's really crazy about me, and she thinks *I'm* crazy for not going out with him. And Emily, my friend Emily Gebhart, says I'm a real bimbo, like some kind of an airhead because I said no to Steve. She did it with her boyfriend when she was fifteen, and she—"

"Well you're not Emily!" Eden sat up. Her face was flushed, not from the heat now but from indignation. "You're not like that. You've got your whole life ahead of you. Don't listen to girls like Elaine or Emily. You're you, you're special. You're not like them."

Kim's eyes had widened. "Don't get mad," she said.

"But I *am* mad. I'm mad because both your friends and Steve are trying to push you into something you're not ready for. And because I'd like to throttle Emily what's-her-name."

"Gebhart. That's her adopted name. She moved here from Canada years ago." Kim began to chew on the blade of grass. "I feel sorry for her, Eden, because she's adopted I mean. It must be terrible to know that your own mother didn't want you, that your own mother just . . . just gave you away."

Pain shot through Eden, pain so deep and cutting that for a moment she couldn't speak. But at last she made herself say, "Maybe her birth mother didn't have any choice, Kim. Maybe she was too young for the responsibility and thought that her baby . . . her daughter would be better off with somebody else, with a couple who would love her and who could probably give her more advantages than she could."

"But to give away your own baby!" Kim shook her head. "That's a terrible thing to do."

The pain dug even deeper into Eden's midsection. She looked away, out toward the water, and bit down hard on the inside of her cheek so that she wouldn't cry. Dear God, she thought. Is that how my daughter feels? Does she think I gave her up because I didn't want her? What if she was like Kim's friend Emily? A little girl growing up too quickly in an attempt to find the love that her own mother hadn't been able to give her.

The thought of it tore at her heart and made her so physically ill that when she and Kim finally picked up their rackets and headed for the restaurant she wasn't able to eat.

But she put aside her own feelings and when she and Kim said goodbye on the steps of the restaurant Eden said, "What about Steve, Kim? Are you going to go out with him tonight?"

"I . . . I'm not sure, Eden."

"It's difficult, isn't it? Being young I mean, and having to make adult decisions." She curled a lock of Kim's fair hair around her finger. "But you're a pretty special someone, Kimmer, and I've got a feeling you're going to make the right decision." Eden hesitated. "And remember that I'm here for you, okay? Any time you want to talk I mean."

"I wish..." Kim dug a hole in the sand with the toe of her sneaker. "I wish that you could stay here forever, Eden. I wish you and my dad..." Hot color crept into her cheeks. "I wish the two of you would . . . you know, like fall in love and then you wouldn't leave. I wish—"

"Hey, Kim!" Elaine, beach bag in her hand, headed across the lawn toward them.

"You'd better go, honey." Eden squeezed Kim's shoulders. "I'll see you soon."

"Wednesday? Could we play again Wednesday?"

"Sure." Eden smiled as Elaine approached, then with a wave she headed for her car.

And all the way back to the white clapboard house she thought of Kim's words . . . I wish you could stay here forever. I wish the two of you could fall in love.

Linc phoned her that night. "I have tomorrow afternoon off," he said. "How'd you like to sail down toward Naples for dinner?"

"I'd love to."

"I'll pick you up at three. Would that be convenient?"

"That would be fine."

"Bring a suit. We might want to swim off the boat."

"All right."

"We need to talk, Eden."

Involuntarily her hand tightened on the phone but before she could answer he said, "Until tomorrow then."

When she put the phone down she went over to the closet and began to look through her clothes, frowning because it seemed to her as though she had nothing to wear. She tried to tell herself that she was being foolish, that of course she had something to wear, her white denims would be fine with the blue T-shirt, and her two-year-old one-piece swimsuit was perfectly acceptable.

But the next morning as soon as she finished breakfast she went shopping. She tried on a pale turquoise bikini, a one-piece white suit, a fairly conservative two-piece black, and decided on the bikini.

She debated over buying shorts and a top, but when she saw a pink-and-white skinny-strapped dress with a low scooped back and a full whirling skirt she decided to buy that instead. After all, they were going out to dinner, she told herself that afternoon when she was getting dressed. And though it was a date of sorts she really must not fool herself into thinking that Linc had asked her to go out with him for any other reason than to tell her that the other night shouldn't have happened.

Of course it shouldn't have. Even now she couldn't quite believe that she and Linc had made love. Her cheeks flushed when she remembered how it had been, how she had held his head against her breasts and how she had lifted her body to his. In the year she had been married she had never experienced the kind of emotion she had experienced with Linc, and the thought that she knew it shouldn't happen again filled her with a terrible sense of loss.

She heard the car pull up in the driveway, then Phoebe Rose called out, "Dr. Linc is here."

"I'll be right down." She combed her hair back in a ponytail, looked at herself in the mirror, then changed her mind and brushed it loose about her shoulders. She put lipstick on, decided it was the wrong shade, wiped it off and touched pale pink to her lips. And finally she picked up her beach bag and with a last, almost desperate look in the mirror, she hurried from the room.

Linc and Phoebe Rose were in the kitchen. Eden heard their voices and when she pushed open the kitchen door she saw Linc perched on the end of the kitchen table eating a hush puppy and drinking a glass of buttermilk.

"I didn't have time for lunch," he said when he saw Eden. "I don't know how it happens, but every time I come it seems like Phoebe Rose has just made a batch of hush puppies." He passed her the plate. "They're good. Have one."

"No thanks. I had a late lunch."

"I've got a Key lime pie in the refrigerator, Dr. Linc," Phoebe Rose said. "Let me cut you a piece."

Linc shook his head. "This is my third hush puppy. If I have a piece of pie I won't want dinner."

"Then maybe when you and Miss Eden come back tonight."

"That'll be fine." Linc slid off the table. "Ready?" he asked Eden, then with a slight smile he said, "You look nice." And though he'd been expecting her to be wearing either jeans or shorts, he couldn't help being pleased that she'd chosen to wear this summery dress instead.

Phoebe Rose went to the door with them and waved as they drove out of the driveway.

"She's a wonderful woman," Linc said when he waved back. "I wonder what she's going to do after you sell the house." He glanced at her as he started into the street. "You are going to sell it, aren't you?"

"No, I've been thinking about turning it over to Phoebe Rose."

"You're going to give it to her?"

Eden nodded. "She's lived in the house for years, Linc. It's her home. It's only right that she should have it. With the money Aunt Jo left her she'll be all right for the rest of her life."

"What about you?"

"Mr. Prentice said there was enough money in Aunt Jo's estate so that I'd be comfortable. I don't need the house. I really want Phoebe Rose to have it."

"That's pretty generous of you, Eden." He made the turn down to the beach. "Have you heard anything else from Prentice? About the adoption files, I mean."

"No. He said it might take a little time. Meanwhile I've contacted a searchers' group. They're people who were adopted and who are trying to find their birth parents, or parents who put their children up for adoption and are trying to find them."

Linc's face tightened. "So you're still determined to go ahead with this?"

"That's the main reason I came to Wiggins Bay." She half turned on the seat so that she could look at him. "You still think I'm wrong, don't you?"

"Yes, I do." His face was angry. "You have no right—"

"I have every right. It was my baby, Linc. If she's anywhere on this coast, I'm going to find her."

"But she might not be here. Hundreds of snowbirds come to Florida every winter. Maybe one of them adopted her." He turned into the marina parking lot. "Have you ever thought of that?"

"Yes, and I know it's a possibility. But I have a feeling that she's here, somewhere in this area. And if she is,

then with Mr. Prentice's help, or maybe with the searchers' group, I'll be able to find her.''

Linc pulled into a parking space and turned off the ignition before he said, ''You're making a mistake, Eden,
one that could hurt a lot of people, but maybe you, most
of all.''

''I don't want to hurt anybody, Linc.'' With her hand
on the door she looked at him. ''But I am going to find
her. One way or another I'm going to find my daughter.''

It was the kind of day travel brochures write about.
There was enough of a wind to billow the sails. Cream-
puff clouds floated high above, and the air smelled of salt
and the sea. Flying fish nipped along beside the boat, and
farther out, a school of porpoise did a pas de deux across
the water.

They sailed for an hour, the sun at their backs, not
saying much because Linc was still angry and Eden was
still defensive. But when Linc spotted a secluded cove he
headed for it and said, ''How about a swim? Would you
like to go below and change?''

Eden nodded. ''What about you?''

''I've got trunks on under my shorts. You go ahead.''

''Okay, I won't be long.'' She went down the steps into
the cabin and when she'd taken her bathing suit and a
towel from her beach bag she stripped out of her dress
and panties. She was warm and eager for a swim, but
when she put on the bikini she had a moment of misgiv-
ing. It was skimpier than she'd thought; there was a lot
more of her showing than she felt comfortable about.

But it was too late to back out now so she pinned her
hair up into a topknot, and draping the towel over her
shoulders, she went back out just in time to see Linc dive

into the water. He surfaced, swam a few strokes, then turned back to the boat. "Come on," he called out, "the water's great."

Eden pulled the towel off her shoulders, and balancing herself on the edge of the boat she arched her arms over her head and dove into the water.

It was like diving into a lukewarm bath, neither too hot nor too cold, soothing and refreshing.

"Isn't this wonderful?" she said when she came up beside him. "Maybe I'll just follow along behind while you take the boat into Naples."

"And maybe you won't." His earlier anger forgotten, Linc watched Eden roll onto her back and ride with the gentle swell of the waves. He was glad that she was enjoying herself. Carolyn had hated the boat and she'd resented every moment he spent on it. The few times she'd agreed to go sailing with him she'd spent most of the day down in the cabin.

"The salt air frizzes my hair," she'd complained. "It makes my skin feel sticky. The sun's giving me a headache."

Like a sea nymph Eden dove beneath the waves and laughed with pleasure when she surfaced. Her eyes were a deep jade green and her cheeks were pink from the sun. It didn't matter that tendrils of her wet hair hung about her face or that her nose was sunburned. She loved the water and the boat, and because she did, he could take pleasure in it, too.

When she swam closer he pressed one finger against her bare shoulder and said, "You're getting a burn. You'd better cover up when we go in."

"I brought some sunscreen but I forgot to put it on. I didn't realize I was burning. That's probably why the water feels so good." She began to swim in circles around him. "I wish Kim had come today. She'd have enjoyed it."

"She had a date with Steve this afternoon."

Eden stopped swimming and started treading water. "I thought she had a date with him last night."

"She did." Linc grinned. "Young love," he said.

Eden didn't smile. She wanted to tell him that the next time Steve came to take Kim out he should throw the boy off the front porch. Can't you see what kind of a boy he is? she wanted to say. Don't let him see her. Lock her in her room. Do anything, but keep her away from him.

But because Kim had spoken to her in confidence there was little Eden could say. She vowed though that when she saw Kim in the morning she would speak to her about Steve.

She and Linc swam side by side until finally he said, "I guess we'd better get back on the boat. I'd like to make it to Naples before dark."

And when they reached the boat he climbed up the ladder and reached down to help her aboard. She came up beside him, dripping wet and laughing, and when she said, "Oh, wasn't that wonderful?" he kissed her. Before she could respond he stepped away and handed her a towel. "Cover your shoulders," he said. "I'll get a T-shirt and you can put that on."

She looked after him when he disappeared below. The kiss had been brief and yet her lips were trembling, pouted, waiting for more. She stood at the railing and looked out over the water. Take it easy, she told herself. Take a couple of deep breaths and control yourself. That was only a friendly howdy-do kind of a kiss. It doesn't mean anything.

She sat in the bow of the boat and began to take down her hair. She dried it as best she could with the towel and fluffed it out with her fingers. Aware suddenly that Linc was watching her she turned and saw him standing in the door of the cabin.

His eyes were steady and his face was serious. He had one of his T-shirts in his hand.

"Why don't you take off the top before you put the T-shirt on?" he said.

Eden looked up at him, then she reached around behind her and undid the snap that held the bikini top.

He knelt beside her and rested the palm of one hand against her breast. "It feels so cool," he said. He looked deeply into her eyes, then he stood up, over her, legs apart, the sun at his back, his face in the shadow. "I want to make love with you, Eden," he said.

"Linc..." The pulse beat hard in her throat. She stared up at him, and with a sigh she offered him her hand.

He brought her up beside him and into his arms. He kissed her again and when he let her go, he led her across the deck and down the steps to the salon.

The boat rocked gently. He steadied her and when he had pulled the bikini pants down over her legs he said, "Let me dry you."

He was very careful with her sunburned shoulders, her arms and her back. He rubbed the towel over her breasts and down to her hips and around to her bottom. He knelt again to dry her legs and her feet, and when he stood he pulled his bathing trunks off and putting his arms around her he urged her to him.

They didn't speak; they only held each other. His body was strong and warm against hers. She nuzzled her face against his throat and feathered kisses up to his ear.

"Eden?" he whispered.

She looked up at him. "Yes," she said.

He kissed her with all of the passion he'd held in check since the last time they had been together. She was soft and womanly, her skin tasted of the sea, and this afternoon she was his to love.

He took her into the cabin and when they lay down together he began to kiss her again—her closed eyelids, her nose and her lips. He trailed kisses down the line of her cheek to her throat, sampling, tasting, and when her arms came around his shoulders to hold him close, he felt his heart swell with gladness because he knew that she wanted this as much as he did.

And oh, she did. Every touch, every kiss, set her on fire. Her breasts brushed the broadness of his chest, and she whispered with pleasure when he nipped her earlobe and licked kitten kisses against her ear. She stroked his back and he put his hands under and around to lift her as he leaned to kiss her breasts.

''I love their smallness.'' He flicked his tongue against one rigid nipple. ''I love it when they harden this way.''

She curled her fingers through the thickness of his hair and gave herself up to his hungry mouth. A flame kindled and grew and like liquid fire it moved lower, warming her, readying her.

He turned her onto her side so that he could rest his head against her outstretched arm while he pleased and teased her breasts. He stroked her back then slowly moved down to her hip and around to her belly. Very gently he moved her legs apart so that he could touch her there.

''So warm,'' he whispered against her breast. ''So moist.''

Eden pressed her head against his shoulder. It was too much. He had to stop. Had to...

She cupped his face between her hands and brought him up so that she could kiss his mouth. "Please," she said against his lips.

"Please what, Eden?"

Her body pressed against his.

"Tell me, Eden."

No one ever had. No one had ever said to him, I want you, Linc. Love me, Linc. He wanted Eden to say it. He wanted her to tell him that she wanted him.

And when she did, when she said, "Come make love with me, Linc. I want you, Linc. Make love with me now," he felt his heart fill with all the love he had to give, love he had never really given before.

He came up over her. He looked down at her sea-green eyes that were warm with desire, and he said, "Yes, Eden. Now, Eden."

He filled her with his manhood, that special part of him, that essence of himself. And moaned with pleasure when she drew him in, when, with a small gasp she said, "Oh yes, that's lovely. Yes "

He had never felt such love, such tenderness. He kissed her mouth, her shoulders and her breasts, and told her how beautiful she was. He felt the press of her hands against the small of his back and he began to move deeper, harder.

It had never been like this before, not with anyone, never with Carolyn. He knew the thought was disloyal and he tried to push it away. But it was true, in all the years he and Carolyn had been married he had never felt this kind of total giving, this sense that a woman wanted to please him as much as he wanted to please her. It was more than surrender; Eden welcomed him. With every sigh, every murmured word, she told him how much she loved what he was doing to her, how much she loved the feel of him inside her. She lifted herself to him because she wanted to be closer, wanted to be one with him, a part of him.

She whispered his name against his throat and her arms encircled his back. "So good," she said. "Oh, Linc . . . Linc."

She wanted it to go on and on, to never stop. She wanted to hold this moment forever in her heart because she was a part of Linc now; she was his now.

He moved faster against her. There was no more time for thought, only for feeling. She clung to him, whimpering with an almost unbearable pleasure.

"Tell me." He plunged against her. "Tell me when."

But there were no words, only his name "Linc . . ."

Everything shattered in a tumultuous storm of feeling. Her body soared against his and when his body tightened and he cried out, she held him, as he held her, while their hearts raced and their bodies clung.

When at last their passion ebbed, he kissed the side of her face and when he felt her tears he said, "What is it, Eden? Is something wrong? Did I hurt you?"

She shook her head and leaned her face against his shoulder. "I didn't know," she whispered. "Until the other night with you, until now with you, I didn't know anything could be like this. I didn't know this was the way you were supposed to feel. You've given me so much, Linc."

He put his hand against the back of her head and felt his own tears burn behind his eyelids because he wanted to tell her that no woman had ever given him what she had.

But because of the secret he had kept locked in his heart for sixteen years, the secret he could never tell her, they could have no more than this one brief summer. She would leave and when she did she would take a part of him with her. And there was nothing he could do about it.

Chapter Seven

He had wanted to tell Kim as soon as she was old enough to understand that she had been adopted. "We chose you because you were so special," he had planned to say. "Because we wanted a baby who looked exactly like you."

Later, when she was older, he would have told her how lucky he and Carolyn had been to have found her. "Other parents take whatever comes," he would have said. "But we didn't. We looked and looked until we found the perfect little girl."

That's what he would have done but it wasn't the way Carolyn had wanted it.

"I was an adopted child," she said. "My adoptive parents hadn't been able to have children when they adopted me, but a year later my mother had a baby boy. The next year she had twins. As far back as I can remember, whenever she and my father introduced us they always said, 'This is Harry, Matthew and Elizabeth. And our adopted daughter, Carolyn.' "

"We wouldn't be like that," Linc had told her. "Even if you were able to have children, Carolyn, we'd never say that."

But Carolyn had been adamant; their daughter was never to know that she had been adopted.

It had been a mistake. He knew that now.

They had been waiting for a baby for almost two years. "You're right on the top of the list," they'd been told . . . and told and told.

It had been Dr. Castillo who had suggested that Linc and Carolyn take Eden's baby. "Eden's a fine healthy girl," Dr. Castillo had said. "And while I don't hold too much with the Fenwells, they're good healthy stock."

But Linc had held back. He wasn't sure even now why he had, but in a way he couldn't explain it had seemed dishonest to him. Eden was his and Dr. Castillo's patient. This was the most difficult time in her life. She was unhappy and frightened, young and so very vulnerable. How could he, as her doctor, treat her as a patient, then as soon as her baby was born, take it as his own without telling her?

He didn't tell Carolyn what Dr. Castillo had suggested, but she had come into the office one day and she'd seen Eden in the waiting room.

"What a pretty girl," she'd said. "But she's so young to be pregnant. Is she married?"

And Castillo had told Carolyn that no, Eden wasn't married and that she planned to put her baby up for adoption when it was born.

"I want that baby," Carolyn had said. "I don't care what you have to do, Linc. I want that girl's baby."

They had gone to the adoption agency in Ft. Myers, and because they were at the top of the list of those waiting for children, it had been arranged. And Carolyn, before he could stop her, had told everyone in Wiggins Bay that she was pregnant.

Four and a half months before she would have had the baby if she really had been pregnant, Carolyn had left Wiggins Bay and gone to stay with her family in Boston.

As soon as Eden's baby was born he phoned Carolyn. Carolyn had taken a plane to Ft. Myers and he had met her there with Eden's baby.

They had named her Kim and from the day he had first held her she had been the joy of his life.

Over the years, Eden's aunt, although he had never asked, kept him up-to-date on almost everything Eden had done.

"She's in her first year at the University of Michigan," Jo had reported soon after Eden had left Wiggins Bay.

A year later she'd said that Eden had married a young student. And though Linc had said that he hoped she would be happy, he'd felt a strange kind of pang and did not understand why.

Later had come the news that Eden and the student were divorcing.

Her aunt went to Ann Arbor when Eden graduated from the university there, and she'd gone again when Eden received her masters in special education. Later she told Linc of a Caribbean vacation and of a trip to Europe.

"I want Eden to come back to Wiggins Bay," Jo had said last year. "I know her memories of the town aren't happy ones, but what happened was a long time ago. She's promised to come next summer."

"Have you told her that you're ill?" he'd asked.

Jo had shaken her head. "I don't want to upset her," she'd said. "She's coming in June. Perhaps I'll be better by then."

But Jo Browne hadn't gotten better. She had died in May; Eden had come a month later.

Now she was here, and Linc was more afraid than he'd ever been before.

Kim was his daughter, his first consideration. He loved her but he had lied to her. He didn't know what she would do, how she would feel about him, if she discovered his lie.

It wouldn't have been so bad if Kim had always known that she was adopted. If she had known, and if she had evidenced curiosity about her birth mother, he might have told her about Eden. But he couldn't do that now. He had to hide the truth from her.

He never should have allowed himself to have become attracted to Eden, but he had been from that very first day she'd walked back into his office. As he'd watched her that day he had found himself looking for the Eden he'd known so long ago. The dark green eyes were the same, and though she was in her thirties now, her mouth had the same sweet vulnerability he remembered from so long ago.

He shouldn't have seen Eden after that first day in the office.

He shouldn't have made love to Eden.

But all of the "shouldn't have's" in the world wouldn't erase the fact that he had made love to her.

Linc leaned back in his chair and closed his eyes. Never before had he felt with a woman what he felt with Eden. She was the perfect love partner, a woman who gave as she received, who welcomed him into her warmth with a cry of gladness.

If it were not for Kim and for the lie he had told, there would be no holding back in his feelings toward Eden. But he couldn't hurt Kim, not even for Eden.

He had to break it off with her.

Eden gazed across the green expanse of lawn. She'd just had a swim in Marty's pool and now she lay supine and lazily content on a padded chaise.

"I'd forgotten how well you tan," Marty said. "Your skin turns kind of a honey-gold, not all red and peely like mine. You look terrific, Eden, but I'm not sure it's all because of the Florida sun."

Marty reached out for the tall cool glass of iced tea on the table next to her. "If I didn't know better, Eden, I'd say you have the look of a woman in love."

Eden took a sip of her tea. "This is a great patio," she said. "When did you have the pool put in?"

"Last year. So who's the guy?"

Eden shrugged her suntanned shoulders and grinned. "Whatever are you talking about?"

"The guy, man, hombre, gent." Marty swung her legs off the chaise. "Is it Linc? Have you been seeing him?"

"I've seen him a couple of times."

"Been out on his boat?"

"We sailed down toward Naples for dinner the other afternoon."

"And?"

"The dinner was just fine."

Marty gave an unladylike snort. "But do you like him?"

"Yes, I like him."

"A lot?"

"You ask too many questions."

"That's what Charlie says." Marty took another sip of her tea. "I know we don't see each other often, Eden, but I feel closer to you than I do to most of my friends. You had a tough break sixteen years ago and I don't think you've had an easy go of it since. I want you to be happy, that's all."

"I know, Marty."

"Linc is one of the nicest men I've ever known, outside of Charlie. His marriage wasn't too great, Eden. Carolyn was a beautiful woman but she was neurotic as hell. One minute she'd be up, charming and vivacious, absolutely sparkling with excitement. The next minute she'd be nervous and depressed. For weeks on end she wouldn't leave her room. It must have been hell living with her, for both Linc and Kim."

She reached for the bottle of sunscreen and began rubbing it on her legs. "I'd love to see something good happen between you and Linc. Kim's already crazy about you. It would be wonderful for her if the two of you got married."

"Slow down," Eden said with a laugh. "Linc and I have dated a few times. That's all. I like him a lot, but..."

Like him a lot? Just thinking about him made her knees go weak and her heart do cartwheel-type flip-flops.

"But what?" Marty asked.

"When summer's over I'll go back to Ann Arbor. End of story."

"Maybe," Marty said. "Maybe not."

They sipped their tea and talked of other things, and in a little while Eden said she'd better leave because Phoebe Rose had asked her to stop by the store to pick up the makings for a salad.

She showered and changed, and when she was leaving Marty said, "I didn't mean to pry. It's just that I can't help hoping that something will happen with Linc. It's time you settled down. And Linc—"

"I know. Linc is a terrific man, Marty, but I don't think he has marriage on his mind."

"Most men don't, Eden. They have to be eased into it." Marty grinned. "You have to help a man know what it is he really wants, to sort of subliminally plant the idea in his head." She closed her eyes. "Marriage, marriage, marriage," she intoned.

Marriage. Eden tried to push the word out of her mind all the way to the supermarket. What would it be like to be married to Linc? To go to sleep beside him at night; to awaken with him in the morning?

Kim would be her stepdaughter. The three of them . . .

She tried to push the dream away. Daydreams were for children, and she wasn't a child.

But she was smiling when she went into the market and was so preoccupied with her thoughts that she didn't see the person coming toward her until the woman said, "Eden? Eden Adair?"

The woman who had spoken to her wore wrinkled khaki shorts and an oversized T-shirt with the words I'm Ready When You Are printed across her chest. She was large, with ample breasts and wide hips. Her arms and legs were covered with mosquito bites that had been scratched and were now angry and bleeding welts. Her dark hair, once tinted blond but now half grown out, hung in limp strands about her face.

Eden didn't know her. She tried to think back to that long-ago summer, to the young people she'd known then. "I'm sorry," she started to say. "I'm afraid I—"

"You don't remember me, do you?" Lips pursed in a frown, the woman said, "I'm Shirley May Fenwell. Dave's wife." She scratched her arm. "I heard you were in town. I…" She looked past Eden and frowned. "You put them potato chips back or I'll whale the hide offen you right here," she yelled.

The child, who looked to be no more than four or five, stuck her thumb in her mouth and started to cry.

Shirley May, zoris slapping the floor, snatched the bag of potato chips out of the little girl's hands. "Quit that right now, Etta Ruth," she said. And grabbing the little girl's hand she pulled her toward Eden.

"This here's my youngest." She gave Etta Ruth a shove. "Say hello to Miss Adair," she ordered. And to Eden she said, "I reckon it still is *Miss* Adair?"

"Yes, it is. I was married but when we divorced I took back my maiden name." Eden took the little girl's hand. "My name is Eden," she said. "It's very nice to meet you."

The child looked up at her. Dave Fenwell's child. Half sister to her own child. Her hair was brown and so were her eyes. Did her own child have dark eyes. Did she look at all like this little girl?

Tension tightened the muscles of Eden's stomach.

"Got any kids?" Shirley May asked.

Eden shook her head.

"Me and Dave's got three." Shirley May patted her stomach. "And danged if he didn't just go and put another'n in the oven." Her mouth twisted in an unpleasant smirk. "I reckon you remember Dave, seeing's how he gave you a little something to remember him by."

Eden sucked in air, but before she could respond, Shirley May said, "He's taken over his daddy's filling station and we're doing real well."

"That's nice." Eden clutched the handles of the cart.

"You come back to stay, or what?"

"No, I'm only here for the summer. I came back to settle up my aunt's affairs."

"I heard she died."

"Yes." Eden began to shift her cart back and forth. "Well...it was nice seeing you again, Shirley May." She summoned a smile for the child. "But I'd better get going. I have to pick up a few things for Phoebe Rose."

"Must be nice havin' a maid doing all the dirty work."

"Phoebe Rose isn't a maid. She was Aunt Jo's best friend. She's my friend." Eden shifted the cart again. "I've really got to run," she said, and with a final nod, headed for the produce section.

She picked up a head of lettuce without looking at it, and filled a plastic bag with tomatoes. As quickly as she could, praying she wouldn't run into Shirley May again, she headed for the checkout counter.

"Oh, damn," she said all the way home. "Damn, damn, damn."

She had just finished helping Phoebe Rose with the dinner dishes when Linc called.

"I wondered if we could have breakfast tomorrow," he said.

"I'd love to, Linc, but I've got a tennis date with Kim."

"Yes, I know." He cleared his throat. "I told her that I wanted to see you, though, and she said to tell you it was all right with her if you canceled." Before Eden could answer he said, "There's a new restaurant, the Conch Shell, down on the beach. We could meet there at eight if that's not too early. I have to be at the hospital at nine."

"Eight will be fine."

"Then I'll see you there." He seemed about to say something else, but after a moment said only, "Well, then, I'll see you in the morning."

She knew that something was wrong. She didn't know what it was but there'd been something in his voice that frightened her.

He was sitting at a table by the window when Eden came in the next morning. She stood for a moment watching him. His face was serious, almost stern, and there were lines around his mouth she hadn't seen before. He was wearing a dark blue knit shirt that fit snug across his chest and shoulders, and suddenly she remembered the feel of his chest against her face, the soft brush of the curly hair there.

Color heightened her cheeks and she tightened her hands around her straw bag.

He looked up. Their gazes met and held. He stood up and when she reached the table he said, "Good morning, Eden," and held a chair out for her.

She was dressed in a pale pink summer cotton and she'd pulled her fair hair back off her face and tied it with a matching ribbon. She wore almost no makeup, and her skin was the color of golden sand.

It wasn't fair that anyone should be this beautiful so early in the morning. The thought came of what it would be like to awaken with her beside him and as he looked at her it almost seemed to him that he could see her fair hair spread out on the pillow next to his, could almost hear the small gasp she would utter when he drew her closer into his embrace. She would be warm and drowsy and her lips would be sleepy soft when he kissed her. She would press close to him. She . . .

He took a deep breath. "Thank you for coming," he said.

She raised a delicate brow.

"What would you like for breakfast? The eggs Benedict are good, so are the seafood crepes."

"Eggs Benedict, I think." Eden smiled. "Kim and I always have French toast."

"That's one of the things I want to talk to you about," he said.

"French toast?" Eden forced a smile. "Look," she said, "I know you've been worried about Kim's not spending enough time with her own friends but we only meet in the mornings. I've suggested we make it a couple of times a week but she insists that she'd play anyway and that she likes playing with me."

The waiter appeared. Linc ordered and when the waiter turned away he said, "She's becoming too attached to you, Eden. She's excited about the fact that we've gone out together a couple of times. You know how kids are. She's already got us engaged. Yesterday she said if I still wanted to go on the Caribbean cruise she'd go *if* we invited you along." He frowned. "She thinks she's being adult. She told me it would be perfectly all right if you and I shared a cabin."

The shadow of a smile touched Eden's lips. "Kim's almost a woman, Linc."

"No, she is not almost a woman. She's a young girl and I'm going to keep her young just as long as I can. It isn't good for her to daydream about something that isn't going to happen."

He saw her flinch and knew that he had hurt her. He wanted to say, I didn't mean it, Eden. I'm sorry. Lord, I'm so sorry. Don't look like that.

He tightened his hands. "I'd rather you didn't see her again," he said.

Her face paled beneath the tan.

"And...under the circumstances..." He took a painful breath and tried not to see how wounded she looked. "Under the circumstances, Eden, I don't think we should see each other again, either."

"Circumstances?" Her green eyes were wide with unshed tears, but her back was straight and her chin was up. "What circumstances, Linc?"

He reached out a hand toward her, then withdrew it. "You and I are getting pretty involved, Eden. I'm not sure that's a good idea. You're only going to be here for a little while and it isn't fair to either of us to..." He tried to look away from the pain he saw in her eyes. "You're a beautiful woman," he said. "You're warm and loving, and I...I could very easily..." He took a deep breath. "I could fall in love with you, Eden. And I don't think that's a good idea."

"Because of who I am," she said. "Or rather of who I was."

Linc looked at her, not understanding.

"Because you believe all the stories you've heard about me. Because it was so easy for you..." She pressed the linen napkin to her lips to try to stop them from trembling. "I was easy, wasn't I, Linc? That's why you decided we shouldn't see each other again."

"No, I—"

"There really isn't that much difference between you and Dave Fenwell. You both took what you wanted, had what you wanted."

His face went white. "Eden, please—"

The waiter arrived with their breakfast. He put the plate of eggs Benedict in front of Eden. She looked down at the thick and dripping hollandaise sauce that covered the eggs and tried to fight the nausea that rose in her throat.

"I'm sorry," Linc said. "This isn't the way I wanted it to work out, but I...I'd prefer that you didn't see Kim again."

"All right, Linc." Eden stood up and started to turn away, but she hesitated, and with a shove she pushed the plate of eggs Benedict across the table.

In slow motion it tilted and fell, upside down, onto his lap.

The waiter gasped.

Linc said, "Oh my God."

And Eden said, "Enjoy your breakfast."

Chapter Eight

The phone jarred Eden awake. Still half-asleep she reached for it and mumbled, "H'lo."

"Eden?"

"Hmm?"

"Eden, it's me. Kim."

"Kim?" Eden sat up and snapped on the beside light. She looked at the clock; it was a little after two. "What is it?" she said, coming awake. "Are you all right?"

"No. Oh, Eden, please..."

Her voice grew faint, muffled. In the background Eden could hear music and the sound of loud voices. "Kim? What's the matter? Where are you?"

"In Naples. At somebody's house." Kim started to cry. "Everybody's drunk, Eden. I want to go home but Steve's been taking something, smoking something. He says he won't take me home, Eden. I called Dad but he wasn't there."

Eden swung her legs off the bed and reached for a pad and pencil. "Tell me where you are, honey."

"I don't know the address, but the street is Norfolk Pine Road. It's a block off Gulf Shore Boulevard. I—"

Eden heard somebody shout, "Hey, Kimmer, whatcha doin'?"

"Listen, Kim, I'm coming," Eden said. "I'll be there just as soon as I can."

"I'm scared, Eden. I shouldn't have come. I—"

Eden heard her gasp. "Let me alone, Steve," she pleaded. "Please—"

The phone went dead.

Eden pulled on a pair of jeans. She was slipping a T-shirt over her head when Phoebe Rose knocked and opened the door.

"What's happening?" she asked.

"It's Kim. She's in trouble. I'm going to Naples."

"I'll go with you."

Eden shook her head. "I can't wait until you dress." She grabbed her purse, pulled out her keys, and headed for the stairs.

"What about Dr. Linc?"

"He isn't home."

"You be careful, hear?"

"I will. If Kim calls again tell her I'm on my way."

She ran out to the car, burned rubber getting out of the driveway, and headed for Tamiami Trail leading to Naples. She had been there once and that had been sixteen years ago. She vaguely remembered that Gulf Shore Boulevard was one of the main streets but she had no idea where Norfolk Pine was or how she'd find the house that Kim had called from.

She got the speedometer up to seventy and kept it there, half hoping a patrolman would stop her for speeding so she could enlist his aid in finding Kim. But there was little traffic on the highway and she saw no sign of a Florida Highway Patrol car.

When she reached Naples she headed down Ninth and when she saw an all-night market she pulled in.

"I'm looking for Norfolk Pine Road," she said to the man behind the counter. "The block off Gulf Shore Boulevard."

"Turn left when you leave here and you'll be on it. Norfolk Pine is down about two miles. You know the number?"

Eden shook her head. "But there's a party going on in the house I'm looking for. I should be able to find it if it's as noisy as most teenage parties I remember."

"Looking for your daughter, are ya?"

"Yes," Eden said. "I'm looking for my daughter."

"Lotta wild kids running around today. Shouldn't let a young-un out by herself."

"You're right about that." Eden headed for the door. "Thanks for your help."

She ran back to the car, got onto Gulf Shore Boulevard, and after she'd gone a mile started looking for Norfolk Pine. By the time she spotted it she'd already gone past it. She swore under her breath, made a U-turn and headed back.

"Okay," she murmured when she did, "which way do I go? Right or left?"

She went right, down the length of two blocks. All of the houses were dark and quiet. She made another U-turn and headed back to Gulf Shore Boulevard and across. She could hear the music before she'd passed three houses.

It was the house at the end of the block. The driveway, the street and the yard were filled with cars, pickups, and motorcycles. She parked behind one of the motorcycles, locked her car and ran toward the house.

The front door was open. Some of the kids were dancing to a blasting stereo, some were sprawled on the sofa, others on the floor. The air was thick with the smell of marijuana.

"Hey, little mama," a tall boy with a skinhead haircut said. "This here's a private party."

"She don't look like nobody's mama to me." The boy, no, not a boy, Eden thought, but a young man of nineteen or twenty, draped an arm over Eden's shoulder. "You lookin' to have some fun, sweet stuff?" He thrust a bottle of tequila toward her. "Take a swig of this. It'll take that worried look off your face."

Eden pulled away from him. "I'm looking for a girl." She raised her voice over the noise of the stereo. "Kim McAllister," she said. "Do you know where she is?"

"Nope."

"Do you know Steve…" Eden tried to think of his last name and couldn't.

"Maybe he's out by the pool," a skinny girl with frizzed-out orange hair said. "He had some kid with him. She was yelling she wanted to go home and he was dragging her out toward one of the cabanas."

"Thanks." Eden began to push her way through the dancing couples, but the young man who'd thrust the bottle of tequila at her barred her way.

"Now why don't you just leave ole' Steve what's-his-name alone? He's probably fixing to get himself a little and it ain't right that you go barging in on him."

A couple of kids laughed. "Jeeze, Tuck," one of them said. "You shouldn't talk to the lady like that."

"I'm aiming to give the lady a little party of her own," Tuck said. "I—"

Eden elbowed past him and headed toward the back of the house.

There were lights on in the pool area. Kids were jumping in and out of the water, some with suits on, some without. Eden stopped long enough to look around and when she spotted a row of five cabanas at the opposite end of the pool she headed for one.

The first one was empty. She opened the door of the second one and a girl shouted, "Get the hell outta here."

Eden started toward the third cabana when she heard a scream. "Kim," she cried, and pushed open the door. "Kim, are you in here?"

Through the half light of the narrow room she saw Kim struggling up from a beach mat. Her blouse was torn and her hair was disheveled. With a cry she launched herself at Eden.

"It's okay." Eden put her arms around the girl. "I'm here, honey. I'm taking you home."

"Like hell you are." The blond boy whose picture Eden remembered seeing in Kim's wallet crawled to his knees. "Get outta here," he roared. "What's going on here isn't any of your business."

"I'm making it my business." Eden, with her arm around Kim, backed toward the door.

Steve got up off the mat and grabbed Kim's arm.

"Get away from her," Eden said.

He yanked Kim toward him. When she screamed and tried to pull away he said, "You're my girl, dammit. Been holding out long enough. Tonight I'm going to—"

Eden's hand lashed out. Steve staggered backward, went down to his knees and fell onto the mat.

"What the hell's going on?"

Eden swung around. Tuck and two other boys stood in the doorway, hands on their hips, angry, menacing. For the first time she felt a jolt of fear because she knew that they were out of control. They'd been drinking, they'd been taking drugs. They were dangerous.

She looked around for a weapon. In the corner she saw a pair of swim fins, a couple of masks and a spear gun. She grabbed the spear gun and with one arm around Kim started toward the door.

"Where do you think you're going, lady?" A young man with biceps the size of a couple of footballs blocked the door.

"Please," Kim said. "I just want to go home. Okay?"

"No, it's not okay. You came with Steve, you go home with Steve. You don't need no middle-aged broad telling you what to do."

"Get out of my way," Eden said quietly.

"Hell I will. I—" He looked at the spear in Eden's hands. "You wouldn't dare," he said with a smirk.

Eden smiled. "Wouldn't I?"

He backed away.

Eden tightened her grip on the gun. "Let's go, Kim," she said.

Kim put her arm around Eden's waist. Looking at the boys surrounding them she said, "Please. This is my friend. I want to go home with her."

"Not right now, baby doll," Tuck said. "Your friend and I are going to have us a little get-together in one of the cabanas. I love her up some, she's gonna lose that mean look she's got." He reached for Eden. "C'mon, little mama, you and me's got—"

Eden swung the spear gun and caught him a glancing blow on his shoulder. "Next time I'll use the point. Now get out of our way." And holding the spear point forward she led Kim across the patio into the house.

"What the hell's going on?" somebody shouted over the music.

"Some crazy lady with a spear's coming through," somebody else yelled.

Halfway through the living room Kim swayed and stumbled.

"Easy, honey," Eden whispered. "We're almost there."

They made it to the open door and down the steps. Behind her Eden heard Tuck talking to a couple of other young men. She led Kim toward her car, got the keys out of the pocket of her jeans, shoved them into the lock, pushed Kim into the car, and dropped the spear gun on the grass before she got in and snapped the lock.

She started the car. Tuck and four other boys surrounded it. She inched the car forward, toward Tuck who'd stationed himself in front of her.

"What're we going to do?" Kim wept.

Eden clamped her teeth down hard on her lower lip and gunned the motor. The car shot forward. Tuck jumped out of the way and Eden pressed the accelerator to the floor.

Only when they were back on the highway did she loosen her grip on the steering wheel. "You okay?" she asked Kim.

"I'm...I'm okay." Kim huddled back against the seat. "Thank you for coming, Eden. I don't know what I'd have done if you hadn't. Steve said we were going to a party and I thought it'd be okay." She swiped at her tears with the back of her hand. "But he started drinking almost as soon as we got there and then somebody gave him some stuff and he began acting really crazy. I said I wanted to go home and he said we weren't going home until I . . .'' She shot a glance at Eden. "You know," she whispered.

"I know." Eden's face tightened. "Did he hurt you, Kim. Did he—?"

"No," Kim said. "I fought and I fought, but if you hadn't come..." She leaned closer to Eden. "He wouldn't listen to me. Nobody would help me."

Eden put her arm around Kim's shoulders and pulled her closer. "It's all right, baby," she said. "You're safe now."

Kim sighed against Eden's shoulder. Halfway to Wiggins Bay she went to sleep.

The clock on the dashboard read three-thirty, but Eden wasn't tired. Every muscle in her body felt strained with tension. Never before in her life had she wanted to hurt anybody. Never before had she had the urge to strike out, to wound or kill if necessary to protect another human being. Tonight she would have done anything to have protected Kim. If Tuck hadn't jumped out of the way she'd have run him down. And yes, she would have used the spear gun on the boy who'd tried to block their way out of the cabana if he hadn't stepped aside.

Nobody had been there when Dave Fenwell had attacked her, but she'd been there for Kim. She'd fought like a mother bear for her cub and Kim was safe. She kissed the top of Kim's head and thanked God that Kim had called her.

When they started into Wiggins Bay Eden woke her. "We're almost home, honey. I know you live on Briarwood but I don't remember the number."

Kim sat up and rubbed her eyes. "Four twenty-five," she said. "It's the big white house at the end of the block." She looked at Eden. In a small voice she said, "I wonder if Dad's home."

Eden's jaw tightened. Where in the hell had Linc been when his daughter needed him? she wondered. He had lectured her about Kim being with friends her own age and he'd ordered her not to see Kim again. But *he* hadn't been there for Kim when she'd needed him.

Had he been out on a date? Had he been making love to another woman tonight? Was that why he'd broken it off? Had there been another woman all along?

A tight knot of anger, and yes, of despair, formed inside Eden's stomach.

"There." Kim pointed to a large house that sat back from the street in the shade of large oak trees. "Dad's car isn't there, Eden. He isn't home yet."

Eden pulled into the driveway. She didn't want to go into Linc's house but she had no choice. She wasn't about to leave Kim alone.

There was a light on in the living room. Eden glanced quickly around, noted the deep beige carpet, the comfortable sofa and the matching leather recliners, and turned her attention to Kim. The girl's blouse was half-torn off her and there was a long scratch on her shoulder. Her face was dirty and her hair was disheveled.

Eden barely managed to quell her outrage. "You'd better have a shower," she said. "Then we'll take care of your shoulder."

"Will you come upstairs with me?"

"Of course I will, honey."

"Okay." Perilously close to tears again Kim put her arms around Eden. "I'm so glad I've got you," she whispered.

Tears clogged Eden's throat. I wish you were mine, she thought. Oh, how I wish you were mine.

They went up the broad carpeted stairs together. Kim told Eden where she kept her nightgown and robe, and while Eden went to find them Kim took a shower. When she came out Eden looked at the scratch on Kim's shoulder.

"I'm just going to put some alcohol on it," she said. "You'd better have your dad look at it when he comes home." She put the alcohol on a piece of cotton and carefully dabbed it on the long angry scratch. "Did Steve do this?" she asked.

Kim winced when the alcohol touched her. "He did it when I tried to get away from him," she said.

Eden smothered an oath. Then she helped Kim into her robe and said, "I know you're tired, but how about a cup of hot chocolate before you go to bed?"

"I'd like that, Eden. I don't think I could sleep right now anyway and I don't want to go to bed until Daddy gets home. You'll stay with me until he does, won't you? I mean just in case some of those boys . . ." She took a shaky breath. "You'll stay, won't you?"

"Of course I will," Eden assured her.

They fixed the hot chocolate and Kim brought out the oatmeal cookies she'd baked that morning. When she and Eden were settled in the circular breakfast nook Eden said, "Did you know any of the people at the party?"

"Not really. There were a couple of girls there from my school but I didn't really know them. Most of the guys were older. I thought when Steve said we were going to a party that he meant in town. I didn't know we were going to Naples. I didn't know everybody'd be stoned."

"Did you . . ." Eden hesitated. She didn't want to put Kim on the defensive but the questions had to be asked. "Did you take anything, Kim? Pills? Crack? Anything like that?"

Kim looked horrified. "No!" she said with a vehement shake of her head. "I've never touched anything,

Eden. Not even grass." She made a face. "Dad warned me that if I did, there'd be no television for the next ten years and that I couldn't date until I was thirty."

"Good for him," Eden said with a laugh.

Kim picked up a cookie and dunked it in her hot chocolate. "Why doesn't Dad want us to play tennis anymore, Eden?"

"Maybe he thought you were spending too much time with me, Kim, and that it would be better if you were with friends your own age." Eden summoned a smile. "I'm a lot older than you are, kiddo. I'm old enough to be your mother."

"I wish you were." The words, though softly spoken, were intense with feeling. There was longing in the pale green eyes, a slight trembling of the sweet full lips.

Eden covered Kim's hand with hers. "So do I," she said huskily. "I'd be so proud if you were my daughter, Kim." Afraid then that the tears behind her eyelids would fall, she made herself smile and say, "If you were, I'd be busting my buttons and telling everybody I knew that we were mother and daughter."

"And they'd believe you. I mean like we have almost the same color eyes and hair. I bet anybody we told would believe us. I—" Kim paused, listening "—I just heard a car drive in," she said. "It's probably Dad. What are you going to tell him, Eden? About what happened I mean."

"I'm not going to tell him anything, Kim, but I think you should. He has to know what kind of a boy Steve is. He's your father, sweetheart. You can talk to him."

Eden started to get up out of the booth, but she changed her mind. Linc would be surprised to see her but she could handle it. Besides, she wasn't going to leave Kim here to face him alone.

* * *

Linc was halfway in the driveway before he noticed Eden's car.

What in the hell was it doing here? Was something the matter with Kim?

He slammed on his brakes, turned off the ignition, jumped out of the car and took his front steps two at a time. His heart pounded hard against his ribs. My God, if anything had happened to Kim . . .

The front door was locked. He unlocked it and ran into the living room. It was empty. He saw the light in the kitchen and headed there. He shouldn't have left Kim alone for so long. Something was wrong. If anything had happened to her . . .

He burst through the kitchen door.

They were in the breakfast nook, dunking cookies in steaming cups of hot chocolate.

"What's going on?" he asked. Relief gave way to anger. Kim was all right. But what in the hell was Eden doing here?

"Are you all right, Kimmer?" he asked.

"Yes, but—"

"It's almost six-thirty," he said to Eden. "Were you out for an early-morning ride or were you on your way home from a late date?"

Eden put the mug of chocolate carefully down on the table. "No," she said. "I didn't have a late date. Did you?"

"Daddy—"

"Later, Kim." He turned his angry gaze back to Eden. "Well?" he said.

"I was just leaving." Eden slid out of the booth. She leaned over and kissed Kim's cheek. "Don't forget to have your dad check your shoulder," she said.

Kim's eyes flooded with tears. "I don't want you to go," she said emotionally.

"It's okay, honey." And to Linc she said, "Kim's had a rough night. Her shoulder needs attending to and she needs to get to bed." Before he could answer she turned and left the kitchen.

He heard the front door close. He heard her start her car.

"What's this all about, Kim?" he asked. "What—?"

"How could you?" Kim's eyes blazed with an anger he'd never seen before. "How could you do that to her?"

Linc put his hands flat on the table. "What's going on?" he asked. "What are you doing up and why was Eden here?"

"She came to Naples and rescued me. That's what she's doing here." Almost too angry to speak, Kim stuttered, "Eden practically... practically saved my life. She...she had a spear and she was going to run over one of them if they didn't get out of her way and...and—"

"Whoa. Slow down. I haven't the vaguest idea what you're talking about." Linc slid into the booth across from Kim. "Let's start at the beginning. You had a date with Steve..." He frowned. "What happened to Steve?"

"I don't know and I don't care."

Alarm snaked through Linc. He remembered that Eden had said something about Kim's shoulder. "What happened to your shoulder?" he asked. "Better let me have a look at it."

Still angry, her lower lip out in a pout he hadn't seen since she was three, Kim slipped the robe off her shoulder. "Eden put alcohol on it," she said, and gave him a dirty look.

Linc gasped. The scratch ran from Kim's shoulder to her elbow and fingermark bruises were already starting to discolor her skin. "Who did this to you?" he asked in a quiet voice.

"Steve. He..." Kim wet her lips. "I don't want you to get mad," she murmured.

"Just tell me what happened, Kim."

She swallowed hard. "Steve took me to a party in Naples. I didn't know anybody there. They were all older and they were drinking and smoking pot and—"

Linc swore under his breath. "Go on," he managed to say.

"He started drinking and then somebody gave him something and he got really spaced-out. I said I wanted to go home but he wouldn't take me. I tried to call you but you weren't home. I called the hospital but you weren't there, either, so I called Eden."

"I had to go to Estero," Linc said. "It was an emergency, Kim. I only thought I'd be gone for an hour or two but the woman having the baby suddenly went into toxemia. I got her to the hospital but I couldn't leave her." He squeezed Kim's hand. "So you called Eden?"

"Yes." Kim glared at him. "You were awful to her."

"I know. I'm sorry. I'll tell her how sorry I am, Kim."

"Anyway, she came after me." Kim's chin started to tremble. "Steve got me into one of the cabanas. He tore my blouse. He was going to..." She turned away from Linc. "You know," she said.

He took her hand and held it between both of his.

"I kept trying to fight him but he got me down on the mat and I was screaming but nobody came, and then Eden...Eden came running in the door. She got me away from Steve and when he came after us she hit him. Then some other boys tried to stop us from leaving and she picked up a spear gun and hit one of them with it and then she held it in front of her and kept it there until we got out of the house. We got into her car and some of the guys tried to stop us. This older guy named Tuck stood right in front of the car but Eden started the car anyway and I guess if he hadn't jumped out of the way she would have run right over him.''

''Good for her!'' He tried, for Kim's sake, to hold his anger in check. But rage unlike anything he'd ever known boiled up inside him. He wanted to go after Steve, wanted to beat him, to smash his face and fix him so that he'd never do to another girl what he'd tried to do to Kim. He wanted to go to Naples to find the boy named Tuck, and the other boys who'd tried to hurt Kim.

God, if it hadn't been for Eden...

''I was so scared,'' Kim said in a small voice. ''If Eden hadn't come after me... if she hadn't...'' She began to cry.

''But she did come after you, Kimmer.'' Linc slid out of the booth. He helped Kim out and drew her into his arms. ''You're safe,'' he said. ''Everything's all right now, Kim.''

She clung to him, then knuckling away her tears she looked up at the wall clock and said, ''It's late, Daddy. It's almost time for you to go to the office.''

''I'll call Dr. McCluskey and have him cover for me. We'll both take the day off and tonight we'll go out somewhere special for dinner.''

Kim looked up at him. ''I'd like it if you'd ask Eden to come with us.''

''Kim...''

''Please, Daddy.''

Her green eyes looked imploringly up at him.

''All right,'' he said, ''I'll ask her.''

Chapter Nine

Linc waited until Kim was asleep before he called Eden. She picked up on the first ring. "I'm sorry," he said.

She didn't answer.

"Eden, please..." Linc rubbed a hand across his face. "Please don't hang up."

"I'm awfully tired, Linc."

"Kim told me what happened. There's no way I can ever thank you for what you did, or apologize for the way I acted."

"Just be sure she never goes out with that little... with him again."

"She never will. I'm going to see his parents this afternoon. I'll make damn sure he won't get away with what he did. My God, Eden, if you hadn't gone to Naples...if you hadn't gotten there in time..." Linc closed his eyes against the thought of what might have happened.

"She tried to call you." Anger replaced exhaustion. "If you plan on staying out all night the least you could do is have someone available for Kim in case there's an emergency."

"I hadn't planned on being out all night. I got a call from one of my patients at ten. I thought I'd be back before Kim came home." He leaned back against the pillows. "I'm so damned sorry about everything, Eden. Sorry about what I said to you the other morning in the restaurant..." In spite of everything that had happened tonight, a rueful grin tugged at the corners of Linc's mouth. "You should have stuck around. I made quite a sight walking through the restaurant with eggs Benedict dripping down the front of my pants."

"Linc, I..." She felt hot color rush to her cheeks. "I'm sorry. That was an awful thing to do. It was unladylike, it was—"

"Justified," he said. He tried to find the words to make her understand, and yes, to justify the way he had acted in the restaurant. And though words were inadequate he said, "This thing between us happened so fast, Eden. It scares the hell out of me."

"It scares me, too, Linc."

"We need to talk."

"I don't think so."

"Kim and I are going out to dinner tonight. She'd like it... We both would like it if you'd come with us."

"No. I... I can't."

He heard the exhaustion in her voice, and though he knew that it was unfair he said, "For Kim."

"That isn't fair."

"For me then. Because I need to see you. Because I need to see your face. To touch you."

"Linc... don't."

"There are so many things you don't understand," he said. "So many things I wish were different. Please . . ." He didn't know what else to say. He waited.

"All right," she said at last. "For Kim."

It was something.

"Good night. I wish . . ." Linc closed his eyes. "Good night, Eden."

He heard the soft click of the receiver but it was a moment before he put the phone down, for even though the connection had been broken, it seemed to him as though a part of Eden were still there, that as long as he held the phone there was a contact, a touching.

Tonight Eden had saved his daughter—her daughter—from suffering the same thing that had happened to her sixteen years ago. He wanted to get down on his knees to her. He wanted to ask her to forgive him. To love him.

But he couldn't. God help him, he couldn't.

He switched the phone off, then the light. But tired as he was, it was a very long time before he went to sleep.

Eden was subdued that night at dinner. There were patches of fatigue under her eyes and Linc knew that very likely she had slept as little as he had.

She wore a dark green sleeveless linen dress that emphasized the green of her eyes. Her only jewelry was a pair of gold loop earrings.

Kim, who seemed almost to have forgotten her ordeal of the night before, was bright and cheerful. She gobbled up her crabmeat cocktail and dug into her lobster with an enthusiasm that made Linc smile.

He'd had a long talk with her when she had awakened that afternoon. She had told him, after a great deal of tender persuasion, that Steve had been pressuring her for weeks to have sex with him.

"I wish you would have told me," he said. "Why didn't you? I thought we could talk about anything, Kim."

"But not about that. I'd have felt funny talking to you about sex." She blushed. "I told Eden though and she said that Steve was being selfish and that he cared more about himself than he did about how I felt. She said that wasn't the way a man acted if he really cared about you." Kim took a deep breath. "I told her I wouldn't go out with him again, but he called me and I thought maybe he'd changed his mind. It's really hard to know what to do sometimes, about boys I mean. Some of my friends have . . . you know . . . and they act like I'm some kind of a retard because I haven't. But Eden said . . ."

Linc had listened, and been appalled because he hadn't had any idea what had been going on with Kim. All this time he had thought of her as a little girl, but she wasn't a little girl, she was almost a woman. And that scared the hell out of him.

Apparently Eden had said all the right things, things he would have said if Kim had come to him. But because she was a woman she'd said them better than he would have.

He and Kim had a good father and daughter relationship, but now, for the first time since Carolyn had died, he realized that Kim had needed someone else, she needed a woman to confide in. He thanked God that Eden had been there for her last night. And he wondered at what strange twist of fate had brought Eden back into her daughter's life just when Kim had needed her the most.

"I like your dress," Kim said, breaking in on her thoughts. "It's great with your eyes." She fiddled with the thin gold bracelet on her left wrist, took it off, and handed it to Eden. "I want you to have this," she said. "As a thank-you for what you did last night."

"I don't need a thank-you," Eden protested.

But Kim fastened the bracelet about Eden's wrist. "Dad gave it to me for my fifteenth birthday. It means a lot to me, Eden, and I want you to have it."

Eden, touched by the gift, felt hot tears sting her eyes. "It's beautiful," she managed to say. "Thank you, Kimmy."

And Linc, watching, had to look away.

It was later, when they were having coffee, that he told them that he had spoken to Steve's parents that afternoon.

"What did they say?" Kim asked.

"They were surprised and shocked. They didn't know Steve drank or that he took drugs. Steve was upstairs sleeping when I got there, but his father made him come down.

"It was all I could do to keep my hands off him," he said to Eden. "I kept thinking about the scratch on Kim's shoulder and the bruises. I had to keep telling myself that I was a doctor and that he was only a boy."

"Did he say anything?" Eden asked. "Did he try to defend himself?"

"For about the first five minutes. Then Mr. Kingsley yanked him up off the sofa and really laid into him. Steve finally admitted he'd had a few beers—"

"A few beers!" Kim said. "He was drinking straight tequila!"

"His mother went up and searched his room while I was there. She found the drugs."

"So what's going to happen to him?" Kim asked. "Is he like grounded for the rest of his life?"

"Not quite," Linc said. "His dad called a drug rehab place in Homestead. He's taking Steve there tomorrow morning. Both his mother and father asked me to tell you how sorry they are about what happened, Kim."

"Okay, but rehab or not, I never want to see him again." She took the last bite of her pie. "I think we need a vacation," she said.

Linc looked surprised. "You want to go on the cruise?"

Kim shook her head. "But I think it would be nice if the three of us took the boat out for a couple of days." She smiled shyly at Eden. "We could go down to Flamingo and maybe to Shark River. It's so pretty around there. We could swim—"

"In Shark River," Eden asked with a laugh.

"No, not there. But there are all sorts of little coves and inlets where we could. We'd sun and take lots of food and maybe go exploring on some of the islands." She looked at Linc. "Can we, Dad? It'd be fun. You haven't had a vacation all summer."

Linc hesitated. He knew it wasn't a good idea, knew that two or three days on a small boat brought people closer. He had to make an excuse. He had to...

He looked at Eden. "We could leave Saturday," he said.

"Please, Eden," Kim implored. "It'd be such fun. I really want to get away from everybody this weekend. They'll be talking about the party, about what happened with Steve. Emily will find out and she'll tell Elaine, and Elaine will tell Sue." Kim shook her head. "I'd really like not to be home when everybody starts calling me."

"I know, Kim, but..." Eden looked at Linc.

"Say yes," he said.

She took a deep breath. "Yes," she said. "I'll come."

* * *

They had smooth sailing the first morning out. A brisk wind furled the sails and they billowed out, stark white against the marshmallow clouds and the azure blue of the sky.

Linc stood at the helm, bare feet firmly planted on the teak deck, wearing only well-worn cutoffs. His long legs were strong and corded with a fine line of muscle. His chest and shoulders were broad and tanned a deep golden brown.

He would have made a fine pirate if he'd been born two hundred years earlier, Eden thought as she watched him. In her mind's eye she could almost see him, plying the waters of the Caribbean, and she felt a certain sadness for men like Linc who had no new seas to challenge. He was a modern-day sailor, with a microwave oven, a television set, and a refrigerator stocked with eggs, bacon, fried chicken and enough of Phoebe Rose's hush puppies to keep him happy for the next three days.

A smile tugged at the corners of her lips. It was too bad, she thought. Linc would have made a wonderful pirate.

The sun was hot. It warmed her all the way through to her bones and made her body feel fluid and relaxed.

"Your shoulders are burning," Kim said. "Better let me put some more sunscreen on them."

"I was almost asleep." Eden sat and let Kim drizzle the oil on her back. "I get so lazy when I'm in the sun." She reached for the bottle and began to cream her legs.

Kim watched her and suddenly she began to laugh. "Look at our toes," she said.

"Our toes?"

"They're just alike. The next-to-the-big toe is longer than the big toe." Kim put her foot next to Eden's. "See? Isn't that the weirdest?"

"Strange," Eden said with a laugh. "My mother used to tell me that nobody in the world had toes like mine." She grinned at Kim. "I'd say this makes us kind of special, wouldn't you?"

Linc massaged his forehead. Couldn't they see it? Hadn't they ever looked at each other and seen how alike they were? They had the same eyes, the same sweetly vulnerable mouth, the same stubborn jut of chin. My God, even their toes were alike!

The fear came again, fear of how Kim would feel if she ever found out that Carolyn hadn't been her real mother and that the woman she'd grown so fond of was the mother who had given her up, the mother who had put her up for adoption.

He knew how Kim felt about adoption.

She was only seven years old when she'd told him about Emily Gebhart. "She's adopted," Kim had said solemnly. "Mr. and Mrs. Gebhart aren't her real parents. She had a different mommy but she didn't want her so she gave her away to Mrs. Gebhart." Her small mouth had trembled. "Isn't that awful Daddy? Can you imagine a mommy giving away her little girl?"

He had tried to explain that sometimes women who had babies didn't have any choice but to give them up. "But that doesn't mean that Emily's real mother didn't love her," he'd said. "I'm sure it made her sad to have to give up her baby, Kim, but sometimes it's the unselfish thing to do, for the sake of the baby, I mean."

But Kim hadn't been convinced. "Poor Emily," she said. "I'm glad I'm not adopted, Daddy. I'm glad you're my real daddy and Mommy is my real mommy."

He'd tried to talk to Carolyn. "We have to tell her," he'd said. "It will hurt her now but it will be worse if we don't tell her and some day she discovers the truth."

Carolyn had wept and pleaded. She'd taken to her bed and refused to eat. "She'll never find out," she said. "The girl lives in Michigan. She doesn't know we took her baby and neither does anybody else in Wiggins Bay. That's why I went away, Linc, so nobody would ever know."

"Her aunt lives here," he'd protested. "Eden might come back some day."

"But even if she does she wouldn't know about Kim. She hasn't any right to Kim, Linc. She didn't want her in the first place."

He thought of the night he had delivered Eden's baby. He remembered her struggle and her pain, how desperately she had tried not to cry out.

And yes, he remembered how he had gone to her room that night and how bitterly she'd wept against his shoulder when he'd taken her in his arms.

That was something doctors weren't supposed to do. They might try to comfort a patient, perhaps even pat a shoulder, but embracing a woman was completely unethical.

But he had embraced Eden. He'd felt her warmth and her despair, and for the briefest of moments he had felt love. Later of course he had told himself that it hadn't really been love, he'd only been sorry for the girl.

But there had been times over the past sixteen years, in a quiet moment on his boat, in his office, or in the night when he lay beside Carolyn, that he had thought about Eden.

Now she was here, with his daughter—their daughter—and he didn't know what he was going to do.

They dropped anchor off Goodland Point so that they could swim off the boat. Kim, the first one in the water, called out, "C'mon, it's wonderful."

They swam for almost thirty minutes and when they finally climbed back on board, Linc went below to pop a beer for himself and Eden and to get a cola for Kim. The sun was setting by the time he came back up on deck and the three of them, still in their bathing suits, watched the sky turn to brilliant flamingo, then fade to orange, and finally to amber-gold.

It was peaceful and beautiful here and Eden was glad she had come. For the first time in a long while she felt as though she were part of a family. It warmed her to pretend that it was so, that Kim was her daughter, that Linc was her husband.

What would it be like, she wondered, to sleep beside Linc each night, to make love with him before they slept, to curl her body against his and feel his comforting warmth all through the darkness of the night? To know that their daughter lay snug and safe and close?

She hadn't forgotten her own daughter or the reason why she had come back to Florida, but in a very real way Kim had helped to allay the urgency of her need, at least for a little while. On Tuesday she had an appointment with Carter Prentice; on Wednesday she would call the organization that searched for parents who had given their children up for adoption, and for the children who had been adopted.

Linc had told her she was wrong to try to find her daughter, but she knew that it wasn't wrong. And she knew if she persisted that somehow she would find her child.

She and Linc had been careful with each other since that early morning he had come home and found her in the kitchen with Kim. She knew he had invited her on the boat this weekend because Kim had insisted, but for whatever the reason she was glad she had come.

In the shadows of night Linc's features were in silhouette; the wide forehead, the no-nonsense nose, and the firm chin looked superbly masculine. His shoulders were broader than shoulders had a right to be. His waist was slim, the black bathing trunks snugged tight around his hips.

She looked away.

When the moon came up, full and fat and butter yellow, Eden and Kim went below and busied themselves in the galley. Kim hummed along with the radio while she put a plate of fried chicken on the table. Eden sliced tomatoes and avocado for a salad, and when everything was ready they called to Linc to come down from the deck.

The dining nook was small and cosy. Linc sat across from Kim and Eden. He watched the two of them while he ate, and listened to Kim tell Eden about her plans for college.

"I've been thinking about the University of Michigan," she said. "I could live in the dorm but Eden and I could see each other on weekends." Chicken leg poised in the air she turned to Eden and asked, "Do you live in a house or an apartment?"

"An apartment," Eden answered. "But it has two bedrooms."

"I thought you'd settled on Gainesville," Linc said with an edge in his voice.

"I know I did but I'd like to see Michigan. I mean I've never seen snow. Eden and I could go skiing and ice skating." She turned to Eden. "Do you have a fireplace?"

Eden, aware of Linc's deepening frown, nodded.

"I love fireplaces. We have one and we use it some-times in the winter. Once when it was really cold, Dad and I slept in front of it to keep warm." She reached for another chicken leg. "I think I'd like Michigan," she said.

A cold wave of fear washed through Linc. It tightened his gut; it hurt like a physical pain. He looked across the table at Eden. He saw the concern in her eyes, the knowledge that she knew he was upset. The tight knot of anxiety eased.

"What are you planning to study?" she asked Kim.

"Probably marine biology. Maybe medicine."

"If you decide on marine biology, a Florida college might be better than Michigan," Eden said.

Linc shot her a grateful look.

When they finished eating Eden suggested that he and Kim go up on deck and she'd clean up. And though they argued with her, she shooed them away, insisting that she didn't mind and there was really only enough room for one person anyway.

She lingered over the dishes and the clearing up to give Linc and Kim a little time alone, but finally Kim called down, "Aren't you done yet? It's fabulous up here."

And it was fabulous. There were no other boats around. The soft slap of the waves against the hull and the gentle motion of the boat were hypnotically sooth-ing. Kim sat in one of the deck chairs, long slim legs stretched out in front of her, and in a little while she yawned and said, "I'm going to bed. See you later, Eden."

"I'll go down with you." But when Eden started to get up Kim said, "No, you stay up here with Dad for a while. I'll turn the sheets back in your bunk so that you can just come in and go to sleep." She kissed Linc good-night, then kissed Eden's cheek. "I'm so glad you came with us," she said. "It's turning out to be a super weekend."

"I'm glad you came, too," Linc said when they were alone. He reached for Eden's hand. "I'm so sorry about what I said that morning in the restaurant. I hope you'll forgive me."

She nodded, accepting his apology. "But I don't understand, Linc," she said. "I honestly don't know why you don't...why you didn't want me to see Kim. You said before that you didn't believe the stories that Dave and Mr. Fenwell told about me."

"I didn't then, I don't now. I know that Dave forced you." He took a deep breath. "And I know the same thing could have happened to Kim the other night if it hadn't been for you. That's all I've thought about these last few days, Eden, that nobody had been there for you the way you'd been there for Kim."

"Then what is it?" She shook her head. "Why didn't you want me to see her?"

He wanted to tell her. He wanted to say, Because she's yours. Because I don't know what it would do to her to find out that you're her mother. Because I'm afraid of how she would feel about me if she found out that I've lied to her, that I'm not really her father.

He wanted to tell her how much she meant to him, and how afraid he was. But he didn't.

He got up and stood looking out at the water. "I love being out on the boat like this," he said. "It's the only place I can really get away from things. I envy men who spend their lives on the sea."

The shadow of a smile curved Eden's lips and she got up to stand beside him. "Two hundred years ago you'd have been a pirate," she said. "You'd have stood at the helm of a great sailing ship in shiny black breeches.

You'd have worn a sword in your belt and you'd have had a beard, red probably, and a red bandana tied around your head."

"I'd have plundered cities and seduced helpless young maidens," Linc said, going along with her story. "And one day, off the coast of Southern Florida, I would have found a special lady, a lady whose eyes were as green as the sea, whose hair was like the sun."

He put his hands on Eden's shoulders and turned her so that she was very close. "I would have taken her, kidnapped her if I'd had to, and I'd have brought her aboard my ship. I'd have taught her all the ways of love and after a while she would have loved me. We'd have sailed the seas together and I would never, ever have let her go."

He ran his hands down Eden's arms, and taking her hands he kissed them. "Eden," he whispered. "Oh, Eden."

She tried to step out of his embrace, but his arms came around her and when he kissed her, her lips parted under his.

"I didn't want this to happen between us," he whispered. "It shouldn't have happened. I..." Hunger raged through him and he plundered her mouth, savoring the hot, moist sweetness there.

Against his bare chest he could feel the hard thrust of her breasts, and with a groan he pulled aside the swath of material that covered them.

They were cool against his chest, the tips hard and peaked, ready for his hands and his mouth.

"Linc, please..." Eden tried to pull away from him. "Oh, please," she whispered brokenly. "I can't stand this. I—"

He stopped her words with another kiss. He tasted, teased and nibbled the sensitive corners of her mouth. He cupped her bottom and brought her tight against him.

Through the thin fabric of their suits she felt the power of his arousal, and suddenly weak with desire, she swayed against him.

"Eden, oh, Eden." His body was on fire, throbbing with need.

"No." Eden tried to pull away from him, but he wouldn't let her go.

He took her mouth again and when she began to tremble against him, he cupped her bare breasts and began to kiss them. "Hungry," whispered. "So hungry for you, Eden."

His tongue circled round and round her breast, teasing and tasting before he grasped one tender peak between his teeth. He held it there, hard and rigid while he lapped it with his tongue. And all the while he urged her closer, so close that it seemed to her that the strength of his arousal must be imprinted on her flesh.

"We can't," she murmured. "Linc, please. You said you didn't want this. You said we shouldn't . . ."

He cupped her face between his hands. "I want you, Eden."

"No. Kim . . ."

"She's asleep. Eden, please."

"No," she whispered. "No." And with a muffled cry she turned and ran down the few steps to the cabin below.

She stood there in the dim light over the table and tried to still the racketing of her heart against her ribs. She pulled the bikini top up to cover breasts that ached for his touch, and took great gulps of air to stem the storm of need that raged through her body.

The boat tipped. She heard the splash of water when he dove off the side, and knew that he was as tortured as she was, that the same need that thrummed through her body thrummed through his.

She leaned against the side of the dining nook. "Linc," she whispered. And knew that she loved him.

Chapter Ten

They sailed into Flamingo on Sunday afternoon. All that day Linc had busied himself at the helm. After what had almost happened last night he didn't trust himself to be near Eden, especially the way she'd looked this morning with the sun on her face, a halter top that snugged her breasts and white shorts that cupped her bottom the way his hands had cupped them last night when he'd brought her close to him.

He looked toward the bow of the boat where she and Kim lay together on beach towels. Kim was telling Eden something and they were leaning close to each other, heads together, so heartbreakingly alike that the breath caught in Linc's throat and the palms of his hands went damp.

The thought of never being with Eden again, of never making love with her again, filled him with a sense of loss and of a grief that was almost palpable. When summer ended she would return to Michigan and that would be the end of it. That's the way it had to be, because of Kim, because if Kim ever learned the truth, if she found out that he had lied to her all of these years, he didn't think she would ever be able to forgive him.

Something deep inside Linc twisted painfully. He looked over to where Eden lay beside Kim and the pain deepened and grew.

He tried to stay away from her for the rest of the day. When she and Kim swam off the side of the boat he said he had some work to do down below and busied himself there so that he wouldn't have to be too close to her, to see her wet and sleek in her swimsuit when she came back to the boat after her swim.

So he made himself work on the bilge pump lift switch. He sweated in the ninety-degree heat, swore when he banged his knuckles and tried not to listen to the sound of her laughter.

They went ashore for dinner that night. Kim wore shorts and a top, but Eden put on her white off-the-shoulder dress that made her tan look even darker. In the few weeks since she'd been in Florida her hair had been streaked by the sun. She looked young and vibrant, scarcely old enough to be Kim's mother.

But she was Kim's mother; he had to remember that.

They had dinner at a window table and watched the roseate spoonbills, the flamingos, and the white ibis come in over the bay just at sunset. The evening was tropic-warm and scented with jasmine and frangipani blossoms. He looked at Eden over the rim of his rum punch and saw her watching him. There was a puzzled expression in her dark green eyes, a slight lifting of her eyebrows as though to ask why he had been avoiding her all day.

I've been avoiding you because I can hardly keep my hands off you, he wanted to tell her. Because my body aches with wanting you. Would it always be this way? he wondered. When she was gone, would he still awaken in the night, his body taut and hard with wanting her?

And maybe Eden understood some of what he was feeling, because when they returned to the boat she said she was tired and went immediately to the cabin.

"Isn't Eden wonderful?" Kim said when they were alone. "Don't you just love her?" Her smile twinkled mischievously. "I mean aren't you attracted to her? Man-and woman-wise, I mean?"

"I know what you mean." Linc put one arm around her shoulders. "Eden's a very special lady, Kim, but I don't think either one of us should get too attached to her. She'll be going back to Michigan pretty soon. That's where her work is, where her life is."

"I bet if you asked her to stay she would." Kim's expression grew serious. "I know that Eden likes you. I've seen the way she looks at you. If you said something, if you told her that you cared about her, that you wanted her to stay with us..." She looked up at Linc. "Don't you care about her? Don't you—"

A sudden gust of wind rocked the *Kimmer*. "The weather's changing," Linc said with a slight frown. "We'd better leave early in the morning." He kissed Kim's cheek, but when he saw the question in her eyes he said, "I like Eden a lot, Kim. Maybe if things were different..." Linc shook his head. And because he couldn't explain, he kissed his daughter and said, "You'd better get some sleep. I'm going to stay up here for a while."

But it was a long time before Linc left the deck. And an even longer time before he was able to sleep.

* * *

The clouds were heavy with the threat of rain when they left Flamingo at dawn the next morning. A brisk wind billowed the sails and the *Kimmer* skimmed smartly over the choppy waves.

They had a lot of nautical miles to cover before they reached Wiggins Bay and Linc didn't like the look of the clouds. He had seen Gulf squalls before, he knew how dangerous they were.

A light rain started in the afternoon and grew in intensity as the sky darkened. Thunder rolled in through the heavy gray clouds and flashes of lightning split the sky.

Kim, who'd always had a cast-iron stomach, relished the excitement of the high-running seas. But Eden's face had a slight tinge of green and he could tell she wasn't feeling well.

"There're some anti-motion sickness tablets in the first aid kit," he told her. "That'll help."

She swallowed hard and said, "I've never been seasick before."

"First time for everything." And because he knew she was frightened he said, "The *Kimmer*'s a seaworthy boat, Eden. She's weathered storms before, but if it gets any worse than this I'll put in at Marco and we'll ride the storm out there."

"On the dock?" she said hopefully, and he could almost see her tightening her jaw.

He smiled gently. "Maybe you'd better go below and lie down."

But Eden shook her head. "I'll be all right," she insisted. "I—"

A violent force of wind hit and she grabbed a stanchion.

The rain slashed hard, taking their breaths, blowing in under the canopy, drenching them with its force.

Linc tightened his hands on the wheel. The *Kimmer* lurched to the side, the masts strained and creaked. "Shorten the sails," he yelled to Kim. "Hurry!"

"Can I help?" Eden asked. "Isn't there something I can do?"

"You'd better go below." He peered through the blinding rain. "Snap on a safety line," he called out to Kim.

But she had her back to him as she struggled toward the stern, walking like an unsteady drunk on the tilting deck. "The safety line," he screamed into the wind. But she didn't hear.

Eden saw the fear on his face. "What is it?" she cried. "What's the matter?" She clung to the back of a fastened-down chair to keep from falling. Eight-foot waves smashed over the boat and across the deck.

Another gust of wind hit. Another wave slammed across the deck. The *Kimmer* listed to an almost forty-five degree angle.

Kim was twenty feet away from him. She swung around to try to grasp a line. But there was no line. She began to slide across the deck.

Eden screamed. Before Linc could move, she ran forward, staggering blindly against the terrible roll of the boat. Her only thought was to get to Kim. She had to get to Kim.

Another wave hit. Kim opened her mouth in a silent scream. She reached out for a stanchion.

But there was nothing for Eden to grab. She was on the open deck with nothing to hang onto.

She felt herself going over and flailed at the air. She fell, rolled and slid toward the edge of the deck. Another wave hit, washing over her. It carried her across the deck, over the edge.

Water closed over her head. She went under, down into the gray depths of the sea, and came up sputtering. Before she could take a full breath, another wave crashed over her head. She came up again. The rain blinded her. A wave drove her back and down. She swallowed saltwater, struggled to the surface, and in a flash of orange lightning saw Linc swimming toward her. She started in his direction but a wave hit her with terrible force and she went under.

Frantic now, more frightened than she'd ever been in her life, Eden fought her way toward the surface, toward Linc. He reached out for her. Their fingers touched, then a wave tore them apart.

Lightning split the sky again. Linc reached for her, grabbed her.

A wave smashed at them, battering, bruising. They went down, arms around each other, legs tangled. She opened her eyes and looked into his. Dark water roiled and punished. She felt his strong legs fighting to get to the surface. She helped, pumping hard with the last bit of her strength.

They came up gasping for breath and she saw the boat. Kim threw a life preserver. Linc grabbed it and put it over Eden's head and shoulders. "Hang on," he screamed above the howl of the wind.

They fought their way to the boat and then Kim leaned over the rail and grabbed Eden's wrist. Eden hung onto the side of the boat. With Kim's help and with Linc boosting her from behind, she pulled herself aboard.

Then Linc was beside her, holding her, and Kim, pale and weeping, had her arms around both of them.

* * *

The storm ended almost as quickly as it had come. The seas were still rough but the wind had died and the rain had slowed to a mean and steady drizzle.

It was very late, almost three in the morning, by the time they made it into the marina at Wiggins Bay. Without even thinking to ask Eden if she wanted to go with them Linc drove directly to his house. Kim sat between them in the front, clinging to Eden's hand.

"Both of you go upstairs and have a hot shower," Linc said as soon as they were in the house. "Kim, you find a robe for Eden. Okay?"

"I will, Dad." She put her arm around Eden. "Don't worry," she said, "I'll take care of you."

A hard knot of pain formed in Linc's throat, and to hide all that he was feeling he said, "Run along and take your showers. I'm going to heat up some soup."

But Eden hesitated. There was so much she wanted to say to Linc. So much she wanted to tell him. Thank you for my life, she wanted to say. Thank you for your strength. And she wanted to tell him that in those last seconds when the water had closed over their heads and they had sunk down into the roiled and murky depths of the sea she had opened her eyes and looked at him. We're going to die, she had thought. We're going to die together. He'd known. His arms had tightened around her and he had pushed hard, taking her with him up from the sea, up to life.

Eden stood under the hot water for a long time, and when she came out and dried herself on one of the thick white towels Kim had given her, she put on one of Kim's nightgowns, a robe and a pair of Kim's fuzzy pink slippers.

"We wear the same shoe size," Kim told Linc when they came downstairs. "Imagine that. And our next-to-the-big toes are longer than our big toes."

He forced himself to smile. "Imagine that."

But inside, Linc didn't feel like smiling. He felt as though he were being torn apart, watching mother and daughter side by side in his breakfast nook, heads together, talking. They were too much alike. *Don't you see it? Can't you tell?* he wanted to shout.

Eden tried to eat but every now and then a tremor ran through her body and when it did Kim would reach out and gently pat Eden's hand.

"You're not going home, are you? I don't want you to go, Eden. I want you to stay with me tonight."

Before Eden could answer, Linc said, "If it's all right with you I'll phone Phoebe Rosc and tell her you're okay, Eden. I can take you home in the morning."

He wanted to hold her. He wanted to put his arms around both his daughter and Eden and hold them safe and close. He thought how it would be if they were a family, of what it would be like if the three of them could always be together.

But because he knew it could never be, he didn't reach out for Eden. He kissed Kim and stood alone at the bottom of the stairs, watching until they went into Kim's room.

Eden folded back the sheets on both of the beds. Kim took her robe off and when she turned to say good-night to Eden, she said, "Come sit beside me for a minute."

Eden sat down on the bed and tucked the sheet up around Kim's shoulders.

"I was so scared today, Eden."

"So was I." Eden tried to smile, but the smile faltered and her lips quivered.

"You were coming after me, weren't you? I saw you running toward me, and then I saw the wave hit and you went over the side. If anything had happened to you, to either you or Dad, it would have been my fault because I'd been stupid, because I hadn't fastened onto a safety line."

Eden smoothed the fair hair back from Kim's forehead. "You just forgot," she said. "It's over now. We're safe."

Kim's eyelids fluttered. She sighed, and in a little while her eyes drifted closed and she slept.

Eden kept on stroking the smooth wide forehead. The terror of the day was still with her, but eased by Kim's caring, her concern. In this short space of a summertime she'd grown to love Linc's daughter. At first Kim had eased the pain of losing her own child, and in a way she didn't understand she had tried to substitute Kim for the love she wanted to give to the child she had lost so many years before.

But it wasn't like that now; she loved Kim for being Kim. For the first time since she had come to Wiggins Bay she wondered if she'd been wrong in her desire to find her child. Perhaps Linc had been right, perhaps she didn't have the right to search for the baby she'd given up so many years ago.

As she looked at Kim a strange feeling of déjà vu swept over Eden, for it was as though she'd stepped back into time, as though she were looking at herself at sixteen. It was almost like looking in the mirror at the girl she had been that long-ago summer.

It was so strange, so...

There was a slight murmur of sound and she looked up to see Linc standing in the doorway, an expression in his eyes she had never seen before.

He came into the room. He stood close to Eden and rested his hand on her shoulder. She reached up to cover his hand with hers.

They stayed like that for a long moment and when Eden stood up he put his arms around her and they held each other.

"You were going to her," he whispered against her hair. He tightened his arms around her. "I thought I'd lost you," he said.

Eden buried her head against his shoulder. She felt his comfort and his warmth enclosing her. His arms were her shelter from the storm.

"Come with me," he said, and arm in arm they went down the stairs. He led her into the living room, to the sofa, and drew her back into his arms.

There was little need for words; it was enough to be held by him, to know after the terror of the day that she was safe.

"I haven't thanked you . . ." The words were so inadequate. "I couldn't have made it by myself," she said. "If it hadn't been for you . . ." Suddenly the fear came back. The waves closed over her again. She felt the cold wet grayness, she tasted the salt and the terror.

She moved closer to Linc. Hands on his shoulders, her face against his throat, trembling, she tried to block out the darkness of the sea. She had come close to death today. She had survived but she needed warmth, she needed to celebrate life.

"Hold me," she whispered against his lips. "Love me. Oh, Linc, please love me tonight."

His body tensed. He hesitated for a moment, then he moved off the sofa, and bending down he scooped Eden up into his arms and carried her into his study. He put her down on the black leather sofa there, and when he had closed and locked the door he came to kneel beside her.

He brushed his lips over her eyelids, her nose and her cheeks. He trailed a line of kisses down over her throat and across her ears. He kissed her mouth and her lips parted under his.

With frantic hands Eden opened the buttons of his denim shirt and felt the warmth of his skin against her fingertips.

He tossed his shirt aside and she curled her fingers into his chest hair.

"I love the feel of you," she whispered, and brushed her lips against his chest.

"Eden..." The breath caught in Linc's throat. She was so beautiful, so without artifice or pretense in her desire. With eager hands he opened her robe and slipped the simple cotton gown off her shoulders. He put his hands on either side of her face and ran them down to her throat, over her shoulders, down to her breasts.

"You're so lovely," he whispered. "So lovely."

He took off the robe and the gown and laid her back against the sofa.

The leather was cool beneath her skin and she shivered.

"Let me warm you," he said.

He came up beside her. He loved her breasts with his lips and with his hands. Her skin was so smooth; like ivory touched by the sun it glowed with every touch of his lips. He took his time, savoring her breasts before he began to feather kisses down her rib cage to her belly.

In the dim light from his desk lamp he saw the faint lines of her stretch marks and his heart filled with love for her and for the child she had given him. He traced the marks with his fingers and brushed his lips against them. For a moment he rested his head there, and felt her fingers stroking his hair.

He touched her so tenderly, so gently. He moved her as nothing ever had. A fire burned deep inside her and she knew it burned in him, too. But passion waited for this brief space of time when he rested his head against her body and stroked her thighs.

Tears flooded Eden's eyes because she loved him, loved him with such an overwhelming feeling that she wanted to cry out with it. She wanted to gather Linc in her arms and hold him and beg him to never let her go.

He brushed a slow line of kisses across her body to her thighs, trailing small love bites, turning her legs so he could stroke the tender skin there. He cupped the apex of her legs and began to caress her there, to gently kiss her there.

Shivers of pleasure ran through Eden and she opened herself to him the way a budding flower opens to the sun. Her hands tightened on his shoulders. She whispered his name, "Linc. Oh, darling, darling."

She caressed his shoulders and ran her fingers through his hair. She said, "Oh, lovely, oh, please," and her body trembled and burst and he knew he had never known such pleasure as came from pleasuring her.

He came up over her. He joined his body to hers and she lifted herself to him, welcoming and warm. She held him close and she said, "I love you, Linc. I love you so much."

The climb to passion began again for her. She pressed her hands against the small of his back to urge him closer, and when he said, "Again, Eden. Again for me," she answered, "Yes, oh yes."

She rose to meet his powerful thrusts and when that final moment came she took his cry and mingled it with her own, and trembled with him over the edge of foreverness.

Chapter Eleven

When Linc took Eden home the next morning he kissed her and said, "I'll call you later." But when she started to get out of the car he drew her back and with his lips against hers he whispered, "I wish I could tell you how you make me feel, Eden. I've never shared what we have shared, not with anybody, not ever."

He kissed her once more, fiercely, hungrily, then he held her away from him and with a wry grin said, "I've probably got an office full of patients, but if you don't get out of the car right now I'm going to take you down to the boat and make love to you again."

"Promises, promises." Before Linc could reach for her she scrambled out of the door and with a wave of her hand ran toward the house, laughing back over her shoulder when he called out, "I owe you one."

Eden was still laughing when she opened the door. "Hi, Phoebe Rose," she called out. "I'm home."

"Are you all right? How's Miss Kim? When Dr. Linc telephoned early this morning and told me what happened it like to have scared me to death."

"It like to have scared me to death, too, Phoebe Rose. I wouldn't have made it if it hadn't been for Linc. The waves were so high. So terrible. We went under once, together, and I thought we . . ." Eden shivered, and rested her hand on the other woman's shoulder. "Linc risked his life coming in after me," she said. "I'll never forget that he did that."

"He said you were trying to help Miss Kim when you went overboard. I don't reckon he'll ever forget that." She patted one of Eden's hands. "Before I forget, Mr. Prentice called this morning. He said for you to call him back."

Eden's heart skipped a beat and her hands started to shake. She took a deep breath and tried to steady herself, but her hands were still shaking when she dialed Carter Prentice's number.

"This is Eden Adair," she said when his secretary answered. "Is Mr. Prentice there?"

"He's in court right now, Miss Adair," the secretary said. "Shall I have him call you?"

"Yes, please. How soon do you expect him?"

"Not until later this afternoon."

"Do you know why he called me?"

"No, I'm afraid I don't. But I'll have him call the minute he comes in."

Waiting would be agony, Eden thought when she hung up. But she didn't have any choice. She'd have to wait until this afternoon.

She went upstairs to change and when she came down Phoebe Rose said, "My sister in Estero just called. She's come down sick and she's asking can I come."

"Of course you can," Eden replied. "I'll drive you there as soon as you're ready."

Phoebe Rose called her sister back, and when she put the phone down she went upstairs to pack a bag. "You sure you're going to be all right?" she asked Eden when she came down. "There's steak in the refrigerator and all the makings for a salad. I was going to bake a pie this morning but I just didn't get to it."

Eden picked up Phoebe Rose's suitcase. "Don't worry about anything here," she said. "Stay as long as your sister needs you."

"I don't like to leave you all alone," Phoebe Rose said worriedly when they were in the car, "but Thelma June's got arthritis real bad. She wouldn't have called me, but she's trying to take care of her two grandchildren and she got so bad yesterday she couldn't hardly manage."

When they got to Estero she pointed out her sister's house. Eden parked in the driveway and a frail woman a few years older than Phoebe Rose waved from the doorway. Two small children clung to her apron, and the youngest, a little boy who looked to be no more than three, said, "I'm hungry," as soon as they got out of the car.

"Lord, Lord," Phoebe Rose murmured. She embraced her sister and the children, then headed for the refrigerator, opened it, muttered under her breath and said, "Miss Eden, could I trouble you to take me to the store?"

With the two children in the back seat they drove the two miles to the local supermarket, and finally, with a car full of groceries they went back to Thelma June's.

"You'd better plan on staying for a few days," Eden told Phoebe Rose before she left. "Call me if you want anything. When you're ready to come back let me know and I'll come get you."

She kissed Phoebe Rose's cheek, and with a wave of her hand got in the car and started back to Wiggins Bay.

It wasn't until Eden was almost home that she realized she was almost out of gas, so she pulled into the first station she came to and when the attendant ambled over she said, "Fill it up, please."

"That you, Eden?"

She looked up.

"It's Dave," he said. "Dave Fenwell. I heard you were back in town. Shirley May said she'd seen you at the store."

He'd changed. The summer tan she remembered from so long ago had faded. The broad shoulders were slumped, the muscles had run to fat, and his belly hung over his low-slung belt.

Eden tightened her hands on the steering wheel. "How are you, Dave?" she asked in as steady a voice as she could manage.

"Doing all right," he said. "Got me a passel of kids."

"That's nice."

He leaned an arm in the open window. "You're looking real good, Eden. Damned if you aren't just as pretty as you were fifteen years ago."

"Sixteen," she said.

"Sixteen." He shook his head. "I swear. Don't the time fly by, though."

Eden drummed her fingernails on the wheel.

"You'n me had ourselves a time that summer, didn't we? Danged if you weren't just about the prettiest girl in Wiggins Bay." He reached in and covered one of her hands with his. "I was mighty proud to call you my girl, Eden."

She moved her hand away. "I'm in a little bit of a hurry, Dave."

His mouth tightened. "What's the matter, Eden? You think you're too good for your old friends?"

"You and I were never friends," she said coolly.

"We was more'n friends, Miss High and Mighty. As I remember, we were what you might call real intimate." He clamped a dirty, grease-smudged hand down on her door. "I was your first, Eden," he said with a sly wink. "I got there 'fore anybody else did and I don't reckon you could ever forget that. You got my mark on you, girl. I gave you that kid you gave away. I—"

Eden turned on the ignition, hit the gas, and tires squealing, she sped out of the station.

Sickness rose like bitter bile in her throat, but she kept going until she pulled in to her own driveway. When she stopped she took a deep breath and tried not to be sick.

Everything came back to her. In a rush of remembrance she was back on the beach that night when Dave Fenwell had pushed her down on the sand. She could smell the beer on his breath, feel his hands on her, his body over hers, hurting, hurting her so bad that she'd screamed.

But no one had heard.

She remembered afterward he'd said, "Now don't that just beat all. Who'd have thought a girl as pretty as you would still have been a virgin?"

And she remembered her shame.

She sat there for a long time, and finally she made herself get out of the car and go into the house.

The phone was ringing when she went in.

Eden picked up the receiver. "It's Carter Prentice," she heard. "I've got some good news for you. Looks like we're going to be able to get those adoption files open."

She closed her eyes. "When?" she asked.

"I'm not sure, Eden, but I'd say we'd have them within a week or ten days."

A week or ten days. Dear God, she was going to find her daughter. She was actually going to be able to see her, to know for herself that the child she had borne was well and safe.

"You'll call me?" she asked. "The minute you know anything, you'll call?"

"Yes, ma'am, I surely will."

Eden stood there, her hand resting on the phone after she'd put it down, unable to move for a moment. It seemed impossible that after all this time she was going to find her daughter. What will she look like? she wondered. Will she look like me? Will she...? She thought about Dave Fenwell and a shudder ran through her because she didn't want her child to look like Dave, like the child she had seen in the supermarket.

The sick feeling came again. She went upstairs and got under a hot shower and scrubbed every inch of her body to try to get the smell of Dave, the feel of Dave off her skin. When she had dressed in white shorts and a red T-shirt, she went down to the kitchen and fixed a salad.

But it was hard to eat; it was hard to do anything, to think about anything except that she was going to find her daughter.

"A week or ten days," she whispered, and closed her eyes in a prayer of thanksgiving.

She had fallen asleep on the sofa when she heard someone trying to open the screen door. She sat up with a start, called, "Who is it?" and padded barefoot to the door.

Dave Fenwell leaned against the doorjamb. "Hey, sugar," he drawled. "Whatcha' doin'?"

"What do you want?" Eden asked.

"Nothin' much. Just dropped by for a friendly visit." He leaned closer to the door. She could smell the beer on his breath.

"I'm a little busy, Dave," she said.

"You don't look busy." His gaze rested on her breasts and slowly traveled down her body. "You look mighty good, Eden. Mighty good. Ole' Shirley May lost her figure but you sure enough kept yours. Yes, ma'am, you sure kept yours."

The phone rang. "I've got to answer that," she said.

"Phoebe Rose'll get it."

"She's not here." Eden started to turn away. "I'm sorry, Dave. You'll have to excuse me."

The phone rang again.

"Goodbye," she said firmly.

"I'm not leavin'." He grabbed the handle of the screen door, yanked hard, and shoved Eden back into the room.

"What are you...?" She gasped, then sprinted for the phone.

Dave grabbed her arm and jerked her around. "All I want to do is have a little friendly talk and maybe a couple of beers," he said.

The phone rang again, then stopped.

"Get out of here!" More angry than frightened, Eden tried to pull away from him. "Damn you!" she said. "Let me go!"

"When you'n me get reacquainted and I get what I came for."

Eden hit him, then broke away and headed for the kitchen. He ran after her and caught her by her hair. She screamed in pain and he yanked her around and slapped her so hard on the side of her head that her ears rang.

"Now dammit, you behave," he growled. "I been thinking about you ever since you drove into my station today. Got so hot I couldn't hardly work. Gonna have me some more of that fine stuff I had once before. You liked it then, you're gonna like it now. You're—"

Eden grabbed a lamp up off one of the end tables and swung it at his head. Dave tried to duck but the lamp caught him on the side of his head and broke with a crash. He staggered back, swore, then lunged for Eden again.

Blood ran down from his forehead. He swiped at it with the back of his hand. "Gonna fix you," he rasped. "Gonna fix you good."

He started around a chair toward her. She shoved it at him and when he stumbled she headed for the stairs. She got two steps up when he grabbed one of her ankles. She fastened her hands around the banister and kicked at him. He came half up over her, slammed his fist against her hands, and when she cried out in pain and let go, he pulled her back down the steps.

Panting with effort he dragged her down to the floor. Eden lashed out at him. Rage almost blinded her and she raked her nails across his face. He hit her hard and she tasted blood.

He fell on top of her and pinned her with his body.

"Dave, please..." Eden tried to focus. "You don't know what you're doing. If you leave now...I swear, Dave, I swear I won't tell anybody."

"I'm not leavin' till I get what I want." He pressed his mouth to hers. She turned her head and he grabbed a handful of her hair. His fingers dug into her scalp and he forced her face to his.

She smelled the sweat and the beer and thought she was going to be sick.

He grabbed the top of her T-shirt and yanked. It tore and he put his hand on her breast. She screamed again. He held her with one hand and reached down to unzip his pants.

This couldn't be happening. It was still daylight. She had to stop him. Had to...

A car turned into the driveway, but Dave, too intent on what he was doing, didn't hear it.

The car door slammed. Someone came up the front steps.

Dave swung his head around. He covered her mouth with his hand. "One word..." he warned in a low voice.

"Eden?" Linc called out. "Eden, are you—"

She brought her knee up. Dave woofed in pain and rolled off her. She screamed, scrambled onto her hands and knees, and getting up, she ran to the door.

"I tried to call..." Linc looked at her. "My God, Eden, what...?"

Almost too hysterical to speak, she grabbed his hand. "Dave," she cried. "He tried to..." She collapsed against Linc.

He put his arm around her. He saw Dave Fenwell trying to stagger up from the floor. Dave's face was bloody. His pants were open and he was holding himself.

Fire seared through Linc's brain and the blood turned hot in his veins. He eased Eden into a chair, and clenching and unclenching his fists he started toward Dave.

Dave tried to skitter backward on the floor. "It wasn't my fault," he said. "Eden invited me in. She came onto me. She—"

Linc grabbed him and lifted him to his feet. "You bastard!" He drew his fist back and hit him. Dave smacked the wall. Before he could slide down Linc hit him again.

Everything else blanked out. There was only Dave's face and this terrible burning rage, this urge to strike out at the man who had tried to do this to Eden again. All he felt was the need to hurt, to wound, to punish the man who had hurt Eden.

"Stop!" Eden screamed. "You're going to kill him." She pulled on his arm. "Linc, please!"

He swung around. He was breathing so hard his sides were heaving. He loosened his grip on the front of Dave's shirt and Dave collapsed at his feet.

Linc grasped Eden's arms. "Are you all right? He didn't . . . ?"

"No," she said brokenly. "No, Linc."

He took a deep breath. "I'm going to call the police," he said.

Everything happened very fast after that. The police came. They questioned her. The sergeant in charge took a look at Dave Fenwell.

"Knocked the hell out of him, didn't you, Doc? I reckon we're going to have to take him by the hospital before we lock him up." He looked at Eden. "Maybe you'd better have the doc take you on over to the hospital, too, Miss Adair."

"I'll take care of her," Linc said.

"Whatever you say, Doc." The sergeant motioned to two of his men. "Haul this bum outta here." And when they started toward the door with Dave, he said, "We're going to put you away for a while, Davey boy. You squirmed outta all those other messes you were in but ain't no way you're gonna squirm outta this one." He turned to Eden. "You're aiming to bring charges, aren't you, ma'am?"

She looked at Dave. She thought of what he had done to her before. "Yes," she said. "I'm going to bring charges."

Linc carried her upstairs. As though she were a child, he tenderly undressed her, and when he had run water in the tub he knelt beside it and gently bathed her. Her lip was cut. There was a lump on the side of her head where Dave had hit her. Her arms were bruised, there was a long red scratch across one breast and both of her hands were swollen.

Sickness rose in Linc's throat and he was filled with an anger unlike any he had ever known before. But he put aside his sickness and his anger. Eden was all that mattered now; he had to take care of Eden.

She lay back in the tub, her eyes closed, and let him bathe her. Now that it was over, all of the strength she'd shown before had drained from her body. Tears seeped from behind her closed eyelids, her bruised mouth trembled.

He had wanted to kill Dave Fenwell. He had always thought of himself as a civilized man, a doctor whose profession it was to save lives. But today he had discovered that beneath that civilized veneer there lurked a primitive man not too far removed from the days when men protected what was theirs with clubs. It chilled and sobered him to realize the potential for violence lay so close to the surface.

When he had bathed Eden he helped her out of the tub and had her sit on a stool while he dried her body and took care of her cuts and bruises.

She winced when he touched her lip and his stomach tightened in empathetic pain. He put alcohol on the long red scratch on her breast and when her skin quivered with the sting of it he covered the breast with soothing kisses.

No one had ever cared for her like this, no one had ever touched her with such healing tenderness. At first she had been ashamed to have Linc see her this way, but the shame had gone and she was so grateful that he was here.

He wrapped her in the robe he found hanging behind the door and though she protested he picked her up and carried her into the bedroom.

"Where's Phoebe Rose?" he asked when he put her down on the bed.

"She's in Estero. Her sister's ill. She's gone to stay with her for a few days."

Linc smoothed the fair hair back from her face. "Do you want to tell me what happened, Eden?"

She reached for his hand. "I had to get gas, when I came back from taking Phoebe Rose to Estero, I mean. I didn't know it was Dave's station. He was... He said things, about what had happened that summer, and I...I got out of there as fast as I could."

"Did he follow you home?"

"No, he came later. I was asleep on the sofa when I heard somebody trying the screen door. It was Dave. He'd been drinking. I wouldn't let him in and then I heard the phone ringing. I turned to get the phone and he...he yanked the screen door open and he...he grabbed me."

Linc tightened his hand around hers.

"I tried to get away from him. I hit him with the lamp. I..."

He put his arms around her. "It's all over." he said. "I'm here, Eden."

Her body shuddered against his. "I was so afraid," she whispered. "It all came back to me, Linc. That other time, the time on the beach when he..." She clung to him.

Linc eased her back onto the bed, and kicking his shoes off he lay down beside her. He felt no rise of passion, only the need to hold Eden, to soothe and protect and cherish her.

Her breath was warm against his throat. Her hands curled against his chest. Her body was tense, rigid, and he knew how hard she was trying to hold it in, to not give way to all of the emotions churning inside her.

"Let it go, Eden," he said.

"I can't. I'm... I'm all right now."

He stroked her hair. "I'm here, Eden. I'm here for you."

And at last she began to cry, great gulping sobs that racked her body. He held her close, he felt her pain and made it is own. He told her how brave and wonderful she had been. He said that he was here for her and that he would take care of her. He healed her bruised lip with a tender kiss and feathered kisses along the angry red scratch on her breast. He touched her with hands made gentle by love.

And though his body tightened with passion he held himself back. Never before had he known such a feeling of tenderness. He wanted to care for her, to protect her and love her.

Love Eden.

And he knew that he was beginning to.

Chapter Twelve

In spite of what had happened, and all of her cuts and bruises, the next few days were some of the happiest Eden had ever known. Cosseted was a lovely word, but it was something she had never been, until now.

"You can't stay here in the house alone," Linc had said the day that Dave Fenwell had attacked her, and after he had phoned Kim to tell her about what had happened, he had helped Eden out to his car and taken her home with him.

Kim had been waiting for them when they arrived. She'd put her arm around Eden and leading her to the sofa said, "Oh, your poor face. How could anybody have done such a terrible thing? And look at your hands." She touched the backs of Eden's hands and her eyes filled with tears. "I hope they put that Dave Fenwell in the electric chair," she'd said. "Or put him in jail for fifty years."

She'd made Eden tea and she'd insisted Eden share her room so that she could take care of her. And although Eden said she was perfectly able to come down for breakfast, Kim insisted on bringing a breakfast tray to her the next morning. After she had plumped Eden's pillows and placed the tray over her lap, she'd sat at the end of the bed.

She wanted to know all about the kind of teaching Eden did, what Ann Arbor was like, and whether or not Eden had a steady boyfriend.

"I go out sometimes," Eden said, "but not with anybody special."

"Were you ever married?"

Eden nodded. "When I was in college."

"What happened?"

"We were both too young." Eden took a bite of her toast. "He was a nice boy," she said thoughtfully, "but I don't think I was ever in love with him."

Kim wrinkled her forehead. "How do you know when you're really in love?"

Eden leaned back against the pillows. "I'm not sure I can answer that. It's probably different for everybody, Kim, but I think it's when you can't stand being apart from someone, when you want to be with him all of the time. It's when you long for the sound of his voice, the touch of his hand. It's the way you feel when he puts his arms around you, like...like it's a coming home, a sense of belonging."

"Have you ever felt like that with Dad?"

Eden had just picked up her coffee. Now she stopped, the cup halfway to her lips. She didn't want to lie, but how could she tell the truth? How could she say, I never knew what love was until your father kissed me? I never knew a touch could mean so much? I love him more than I ever thought it was possible to love?

"Kim..." Eden took a deep breath. "Your father's a wonderful man," she said. "Maybe if I lived here..." She put her coffee cup back on the saucer. "But I don't, Kim. I have a job—"

"You could get a job here. You and Dad could see each other and then maybe you'd be sure how you felt about him."

"Kim, I—"

"I don't want you to leave, Eden. Dad's wonderful and I love him. But it's different with you. You're a woman, we can talk about things. I used to try to talk to my mother but she was sick so much of the time. I never talked to her like I talk to you. Sometimes I tried but when I did she'd look upset and she'd tell me not to be silly or to go and talk to Dad. Like when I got my period. I was scared because she hadn't explained anything to me and when I had cramps I thought something was wrong. I was embarrassed. You know? And she said that I should talk to Dad because he was a doctor and she wasn't."

Kim clasped her hands together across her knees. "I feel like I can tell you anything, Eden. I can say anything and you won't think I'm dumb."

"Because you're not dumb." Eden sat up and reached for Kim's hand. "You're kind and brave and wonderful. And I'd give anything in the world if you were my daughter."

A slow smile started at the corners of Kim's lips. "If you and Dad got married I would be," she said. "Maybe you ought to give it some thought."

Eden looked startled, then she shook her head and with a laugh she said, "Shut up and dunk your doughnut."

But Kim wasn't about to shut up. The next morning she put Linc's coffee in front of him and in an innocent voice said, "It's nice having Eden here, isn't it?"

"Yes, it is, Kim. I appreciate that you're taking such good care of her."

"I like to. Eden's wonderful. I hate what that terrible Mr. Fenwell did to her."

That terrible Mr. Fenwell, Linc thought. Your father.

For the first time in his life Linc was glad that Carolyn had gone through the charade of making everyone in Wiggins Bay believe that she was pregnant. No one in town even suspected that Kim had been adopted. As far as everybody knew Carolyn had gone to Boston to visit her parents and she'd had the baby there.

He had hated the deception, and he'd hated lying to Kim. Now he thanked God that they'd lied and that Kim would never know that Dave Fenwell was her real father.

But he isn't her father, Linc thought. I am. And I'll do anything I have to to keep her from ever knowing the truth.

"I wish Eden didn't have to go back to Michigan next month," Kim said. "I wish she could stay here with us."

Linc shifted uncomfortably. "Eden has a job she has to go back to, Kim."

"That's what she said, too." She put a glass of orange juice in front of him. "I'd like to ask you a personal question," she said. "Do you think if Eden stayed around for a while that you might fall in love with her?"

He almost choked on his orange juice, but before he could answer, Kim said, "Maybe it's time you thought about getting married again, Dad. I want you to know that I wouldn't mind if you did. I mean, if you married someone like Eden." She grinned. "Well actually I wouldn't mind if you married Eden."

He was afraid if he looked at her she would see his shock. He wasn't sure how this had happened or why his daughter had become so attached to the woman who was her mother. Was it biological, an innate feeling of a natural love that could not be denied? Flesh of my flesh, bone of my bone? A child born of a woman who for one brief moment had lain on her mother's breast? Was it possible for a bonding to take place in that moment? And what force of nature, of destiny or of God had brought them together again?

With a terrible effort, trying not to show all of the emotions that were tearing him apart, Linc said, "I'm very fond of Eden, Kim, but she's only been here for a few weeks. We really haven't had a chance to get awfully well acquainted. We—"

"But you said you knew her before."

"She was a patient of mine then. That's a little different than really knowing somebody."

"What was wrong with Eden? Why were you taking care of her?"

"It was a long time ago," he said. "I don't remember."

"Maybe if the two of you took a cruise together..."

"Kim—"

"Ships are romantic places, Dad. You could walk on the deck in the moonlight, make love—"

"Now wait just a damn minute," Linc said in his toughest I'm-the-parent-you're-the-child voice.

"It's what people do when they're in love," she said patiently, and with a wicked smile added, "besides, it's probably good for the cholesterol."

He slid out of the booth.

"I just wanted you to know how I feel, about Eden. I wouldn't want you *not* to get married because of me. Okay?"

"Okay," Linc said. "I read you loud and clear. Now butt out."

Kim's smile was sweetly innocent. "Of course, Daddy," she said. "Whatever you say."

It was almost seven when Linc got home that night. He'd had an unusually busy day at the office, three patients that he'd had to see at the hospital and an emergency C-section. He wanted a long cool shower, a drink, and a quiet dinner.

Eden was alone in the living room when he came in. Her bruises had faded and the cut on her lip had healed. She had on a light blue denim skirt and an off-the-shoulder blue blouse. Her blond hair curled softly around her shoulders. She looked fresh and young and beautiful.

"Hi." She put down the book she'd been reading. "You look tired. Rough day?"

"Rough enough." He took his jacket off and hung it over a chair. "Where's Kim?"

"At Elaine's. They were going to a movie and Kim's going to spend the night with her."

"Spend the night?" Linc frowned. "She doesn't do that unless she tells me first."

"Didn't she call you? She said she was going to."

"I spent most of the afternoon at the hospital."

"Then she must have missed you. She's been stuck in the house with me for the last four days, Linc. She needed to get out and have some fun."

"Yes, but..." But he had a sneaking suspicion that Kim had planned to spend the night with Elaine so that he and Eden would be alone. That both chagrined and embarrassed him. "I'll call her at Elaine's," he said.

Eden glanced at her watch. "She's probably at the movie by now, Linc. Look, why don't you have a shower while I start dinner. Kim told me you liked scampi and she bought some shrimp for dinner. It won't take me long to fix it."

"Are you up to cooking?"

"Of course I am. I called Phoebe Rose today. Her sister's better and I'm going to Estero to pick her up tomorrow." Eden smiled at him. "You and Kim have been wonderful to me, Linc. She's a terrific girl. You must be so proud of her."

"I am," he said, though at the moment he'd have liked to throttle her.

By the time he came out of the shower his anger had faded and he'd started looking forward to an evening alone with Eden. He hummed while he toweled his hair dry and splashed a lime-scented aftershave on his face. He put on a pair of white shorts, pulled a black T-shirt over his head, and slipped huaraches on his feet.

She smiled at him when he went into the kitchen and his temperature hit a hundred and six.

"There's a nice breeze tonight," she said. "I've made drinks. I thought we could have them out on the patio. You go ahead, I'll bring everything out."

Linc nodded as he opened the French doors and went out to the garden.

He had bought the house eighteen years ago because of the garden and it was still his pride and joy. Crimson bougainvillea grew up one side of the house, crotons and hibiscus lined the garden paths. Mango, avocado, and grapefruit trees grew at the end of the yard, and it had always given him a particular kind of pleasure to be able to pick the fruit off his own trees.

He'd planted the azaleas, the meadow-beauties, the amaryllis, the bird of paradise and the jasmine. Three years ago Kim had put in a rose garden.

He stretched out on the chaise and sighed. It was that special time of night when the heat of the day diminished and everything stilled. It was good to be home and know that, at least for tonight, Eden was here with him.

When she came out into the yard she put a tray with two frosty glasses, chips, and a bowl of guacamole on the table between them.

"It's lovely here," she said.

"Yes." He wished it could always be like this, that every night for the rest of his life he would find her here—lovely, feminine, welcoming. He wanted to sit in this quiet garden with her for the next fifty years. He wanted to live with her and grow old with her. He wanted to make love with her every night for the rest of their lives.

They sipped their drinks and listened to the birds come to roost in the acacia tree. A half-moon rose, and still they lingered, speaking softly, listening to the sounds of the night. And finally Eden went in to fix the scampi.

It was a perfect meal. The tablecloth was pristine white, the candles were pink. When Linc told her how good everything was she said, "Pure luck. I haven't made scampi in years. We can't get the kind of shrimp in Michigan you have here. I never bother fixing it for myself."

"What about your gentleman callers?"

"They're few and far between." She passed the basket of garlic bread. "I've been so busy working the last couple of years that about all I do when I get home is pop a frozen dinner in the oven. I've almost forgotten how to cook."

"Almost but not quite." Linc bit into a shrimp. "This is wonderful," he said.

"It's my farewell dinner. I'm sorry Kim isn't here."

Linc reached across the table and took her hand. "I love my daughter more than anything in the world," he said. "But it's awfully nice to be able to spend an evening alone with you."

Her face in the soft glow of the candles was indescribably beautiful. He wished that she were his wife. He wished that she would never leave him.

They took their coffee and their dessert—apple pie with warm melted cheese over it—out to the patio. When they had settled into the chaises Eden said, "It must have been lovely for Kim, growing up here. She must have had a wonderful childhood."

Linc hesitated. In a way he could not explain he wanted Eden to know how it had been, for Kim and for him. He had taken her child; it seemed to him that she had a right to know.

"It wasn't all that great, Eden," he said after a moment of reflection. "Carolyn was ill a lot of the time. She was nervous, high-strung, and she was a perfectionist." Linc looked at Eden through the darkness. "She didn't want Kim to touch her things. If she had flowers in the house Kim wasn't allowed to touch them, or her plants, or her collection of crystal figures. There was one piece that Kim especially loved, of a shepherd girl with a lamb over her shoulder.

"When she was four or five she would stand with her hands behind her back looking at it.

"One day the temptation to touch it was more than she could resist. She picked it up just as Carolyn came into the room. Carolyn saw her and she screamed. That scared Kim and Kim dropped it. Before I could stop her, Carolyn had grabbed a ruler off the desk and started beating the backs of Kim's hands." He hesitated. "She . . . she broke one of Kim's fingers, Eden."

"Oh no." Eden gasped, sickened at the thought of a child being brutalized.

"Carolyn was sorry of course, so sorry that she took to her bed for a week. And Kim . . ." Linc shook his head. "Kim tiptoed around the house for days, looking subdued and guilty."

He turned to Eden. "She didn't have an easy time of it," he said with a sigh. "She could never have friends over. She couldn't play the stereo I bought for her. She felt responsible every time Carolyn became ill, as though in some way, by something she had said or done, she had made her ill. I should have done something, Eden. I should have made things better for her. I went to all of the school plays and parents' night, things like that. But I should have done more."

"Didn't Carolyn do any of those things?"

"She said they made her nervous. She couldn't cope. She couldn't cope with anything."

"I'm so sorry, Linc."

"Maybe it was my fault." For a few moments he didn't speak, but finally he allowed himself to say, "I didn't love her, Eden. I thought I did when we were first married. She was twenty and I was twenty-two. I was doing my residency at Jackson in Miami and my hours were terrible. Most of the time I was on twenty-four-hour call.

When I had a night off I was so damn tired all I wanted to do was sleep.''

"But weren't things better later? I mean after you came here and went into practice? After Kim was born?''

"No," he said. "No, it was never better.''

He reached for Eden's hand and when he had enfolded it in his he said, "Carolyn and I were married for a long time, Eden. But in all those years I never shared with her what I have shared with you. I never felt for her what I feel with you.''

He caressed the back of her hand with his thumb. "I came close to falling in love with you a long time ago,'' he said. "It happened that night at the hospital, after you'd had your baby, the night I held you in my arms. You were so young, only a little older than Kim is now, and you'd suffered so much. I knew you were hurting, knew that a part of your life had been torn from you. I wanted to help you, to hold you and love you, but there wasn't anything I could do.''

"I used to think about that night," Eden said softly. "I remember your strength, Linc, and your compassion. It was strange because I didn't want it to be you who delivered my baby, but when the pains came I knew you were there for me. I knew that together we wouldn't let anything happen to my baby.''

Linc closed his eyes. "I wish things could have been different," he murmured. "I wish..." He shook his head, and because he knew they were on dangerous ground he made himself smile and say, "You know, I used to sit out here alone at night and wonder what it would be like to make love in the garden.''

"Under the azalea bushes." Eden squeezed his hand. A flood of tenderness welled up inside her. She wanted to reach out to Linc, wanted in some way to make up for all the unhappy times he'd ever had, and for all the years she had spent without him.

She swung her legs off the chaise and came to sit beside him. "I've never made love in a garden," she said.

He felt the breath stop in his throat.

She began to unbutton her blouse, and when she had taken it off, she dropped it onto the grass.

Moonlight stroked her breasts. Her eyes were soft, her lips tremulous.

His body tightened with desire.

They undressed each other and together they lay back on the chaise. It was enough for now to hold each other and to listen to the call of the night birds in the trees above them. Her skin was smooth, cool and lightly scented. He rested his face against her throat and when she began to stroke his shoulders and his back he sighed with pleasure.

This is the way love was meant to be, he thought, the way love is when it's fine and good. There was no yesterday, no tomorrow, only now and Eden and the way he felt when they were together.

Her hands were soft against his skin. They curled through his chest hair, soothing and exciting him. She stroked down over his hips and across his stomach, and when she reached the apex of his legs she began to caress him, lightly, lovingly.

He kissed her with a hunger he had never known before. I'll never get enough of her, a voice inside his head cried out. It will never be enough.

He caressed her moon-kissed breasts and she drew closer. The peaks, like small succulent berries, waited for his touch, so he took one between his teeth to sample and to taste and her body quivered with pleasure.

"Yes," she whispered. "Like that, yes."

They lay facing each other, legs entwined, close and loving. Bodies pressed together and they kissed again and again, tender kisses, fierce kisses, and when they both began to tremble with need Eden broke away long enough to say, "There isn't room on the chaise, Linc."

Disappointment stabbed through him, but before he could say anything, Eden moved off the chaise onto the grass and held out her arms to him.

The grass was damp with dew but it didn't matter. Nothing mattered except the wonder of his body over hers, the whole wonderful masculine length of him against her.

The night was perfumed with jasmine and orchestrated with bird songs when they came together. He began to move against her, he filled her, he pleased her, he did everything for her.

"I want to look at you," he murmured. "I want to see your face." He held her and rolled her on top of him.

Her naked body gleamed like golden sand in the moonlight, her fair hair streamed over her shoulders and her breasts. It splayed across his chest like strands of pure silk.

"Tell me how I make you feel," he said.

"I love what you do to me," she whispered. "I love you inside me. I love your hands on me, your mouth on me."

He kissed her breasts. "Like this?" he whispered. "Like this, Eden?"

"Ahh, Linc." Her body arched and she began to move against him. He held her there, urging her on until she thought her body would surely burst with pleasure.

When it did, she cried his name and held tightly to his shoulders for fear that if she didn't she would spin off into the night. And when his body arched under hers she collapsed over him. She took his cry, she took his breath. "I love you," she whispered. "I love you, Linc."

"And I love you."

They lay on their backs on the dew-wet grass and looked up through the tree tops to the stars.

He had never known such peace. His body felt cleansed of all tension, all stress. Never before had there been a night like this. The moon had never shone as brightly, there had never been so many stars. Love had never been so good.

In a little while they took their clothes and went in. And after they had showered they made love again, this time in his bed.

And went to sleep at last, close and loving in each other's arms.

Chapter Thirteen

They were having breakfast the next morning when Kim called. "Elaine and I are going to the club," she told her father. "Is everything all right there?"

"Everything's fine. Why didn't you tell me you planned to spend the night with Elaine?"

"Well . . . we, uh, just sort of decided at the last minute."

"You didn't call me."

"I tried. Your line was busy. But I told Eden. Is she there? May I speak to her?"

"Okay, Kim. But after this, you check with me when you're not going to be home." He handed the phone to Eden. "Kim wants to talk to you," he said.

"How was dinner?" Kim asked when Eden came on the line.

"Just fine, thanks to you. The shrimp were wonderful."

"Did you use the candles I bought?"

"Of course," Eden said with a smile.

"And you had a nice evening?"

"Very nice."

"And now you and Dad are having breakfast and everything's okay, with you and Dad, I mean?"

"Everything's fine. How was the movie?"

"Okay. Nothing special. Will I see you later?"

"Maybe not today, Kim. Phoebe Rose called so I'm going to Estero to pick her up. I'll call you later."

"You're leaving? You won't be staying with us anymore?"

"I loved being your roommate, Kim, but I've really got to go back to the house."

"Well, call me, okay?"

"Of course I will, honey. Take care now."

When she put the phone down Linc said, "She didn't want you to leave?"

Eden shook her head.

"Neither do I." He reached for her hand and pulled her into the breakfast nook beside him. "Thank you for last night," he said.

"The pleasure was all mine."

"Not all of it." He kissed her, and because he knew that if he didn't stop he'd never get to his office, he let her go and said, "Dinner tonight?"

"Lovely. Ask Kim to come along."

"I will." Linc slid out of the booth. "I'll call you from the hospital later." He kissed the tip of her nose. "Leave the dishes," he said. "Mrs. Parkins will do them when she comes in."

But after he had gone, Eden washed the dishes and cleaned up the kitchen before she left to pick up Phoebe Rose.

It was a typical south Florida day. There had been a shower during the night and this morning the air was fragrant and clean. The sun was shining and though the temperature was in the high eighties Eden turned off the air-conditioning and opened the windows. She loved the early mornings here, the look of Florida, the smell of it.

She felt so good this morning, so joyful. For the first time in her life she was in love and it was the most wonderful feeling in the world. She didn't know what was going to happen, but for now, for today, it was enough just to love Linc, and to know that he loved her. She turned on the radio and sang along with it, so happy that she almost missed the turnoff for Estero.

Phoebe Rose was waiting for her when she got to Thelma June's. She hugged Eden, then kissed her sister and the grandchildren goodbye.

"Lord, Lord," she said, when she got into the car. "I love those little children but they like to have run my legs off. I feel sorry for poor Thelma June, taking care of those two is a full-time job."

"Where are their parents?"

"Their mama, Thelma June's daughter, died and their no-count daddy ran off. He—" She stared at Eden's arm. "Where'd you get that bruise?" she asked.

"I had a little problem while you were gone."

"What kind of a problem?"

Eden hesitated. By now, half the town knew that Dave Fenwell was in jail and why. The next time Phoebe Rose went shopping she'd hear about it.

"Dave Fenwell came to see me," she said. "When I wouldn't let him in, he yanked the door open. He got a little rough."

Phoebe Rose uttered a word that Eden didn't think she knew. "They should have locked that good-for-nothing lowlife up years ago. How'd you get away from him?"

"Linc came to the house. If he hadn't . . ." She shook her head. "Linc beat him up pretty badly," she said.

"Good for him. They going to send that white trash up to Raiford?"

"It'll depend on what happens at the trial."

"Are you going to testify?"

"You bet I am." It wasn't something Eden was looking forward to but she'd be damned if she'd let Dave get away with what he'd done. Not this time.

"It probably won't be for three or four months. I'll be back in Ann Arbor by then but I'll arrange to come back for the trial."

"I hope they give him fifty years," Phoebe Rose said.

And Eden smiled because that was exactly what Kim had said.

When at last they pulled into the driveway Phoebe Rose sighed. "It's good to be home, Miss Eden." She shook her head and her eyes were sad. "I reckon that's how I've always thought of this house. Thelma June wants me to come live with her after you sell it and I reckon that's what I'll do."

Eden turned off the ignition. "I'm not going to sell the house," she said.

"You planning to stay here? To live here?" A big smile spread over Phoebe Rose's face. "That's just fine, Miss Eden. Fine. I never thought you would. I—"

"No, I'm not going to stay, Phoebe Rose." Eden covered the other woman's hand with hers. "I want you to have the house. I'm going to see Mr. Prentice in a day or two and we'll take care of all the paperwork. The deed will be in your name. It's your house now."

Phoebe Rose stared at Eden. Tears filled her eyes. "You can't do that," she said. "The house belongs to you, Miss Eden. You can sell it for a lot of money. You—"

"I don't need the money. If you decide to sell, that'll be all right. It's yours to do whatever you want to do with it."

"I'll never sell." Phoebe Rose wiped her eyes. "You're a good woman, Miss Eden," she said. "There's no way I can ever thank you."

"You can thank me by letting me stay when I come back for the trial. And by fixing fried chicken and hush puppies when I do." Eden started out of the car. "I bet you're hungry," she said. "I've got the makings for sandwiches. I'll fix something while you unpack and we'll have lunch together."

But as it turned out, Eden didn't have lunch with Phoebe Rose. She had just started fixing the sandwiches when the phone rang and when she answered Marty said, "Eden? Can we meet for lunch? I've got something I want to show you. I think it's important."

"What is it?"

"Some old photographs. I'd forgotten all about them but last night I was looking through an album I didn't even remember I had. There were pictures of you and me and some of the kids. It's . . . it's really strange, Eden."

"What's strange?"

"You'll see for yourself. Can you meet me at the Shrimp Bucket at one?"

Eden glanced at her watch. "One is fine," she said.

And wondered when she put the phone down what could possibly be so strange about a bunch of old photographs.

* * *

Marty was waiting for her when she arrived at the restaurant. "I ordered Bloody Marys," she said. "That okay?"

"Fine." Eden smiled across the table at her friend. "Did you bring the pictures?"

"Yes." Marty picked up the menu. "But let's order first. The shrimp and avocado salad is great here."

"Then that's what I'll have."

Marty ordered their salads and when the waiter turned away she reached into her purse and took out a five-by-seven manila envelope. Instead of handing it to Eden she withdrew one photograph and slid it across the table toward Eden. "This one first," she said.

Eden picked it up. "I didn't know you had a picture of Kim," she said.

"I don't." Marty hesitated. "That isn't Kim, Eden, that's a picture of you."

"Me?" Eden's expression was puzzled. "This isn't me, Marty. It's Kim."

"Turn the picture over. Look at the date on the back."

Still puzzled, Eden turned the photograph over. "June 1975," was stamped on the back.

"It's me?" she whispered.

She was standing at the edge of the beach, ankle-deep in the water, squinting against the sun. Her sun-blond hair, caught by a breeze, blew loose about her shoulders. She was sixteen.

It was like looking at a photograph of Kim.

Her hands began to shake. Her mouth went dry.

Marty reached across the table to touch her hand. "Take it easy," she said. "I shouldn't have sprung it on you like that, Eden. I'm sorry. I couldn't believe it when I saw the pictures last night. I knew it was you but you looked so much like Kim looks today. She could have been your daughter. You—''

"Tell me about Carolyn McAllister," Eden suddenly said. "Tell me about when she was pregnant."

"Eden, look. I—''

"Tell me," Eden said. "Was she pregnant at the same time I was?"

"God, Eden, we were just kids. It was a long time ago. I don't remember."

"Think, Marty."

Marty took a sip of her drink. "She didn't have the baby here. I do remember that."

"What do you mean?"

"She went away. I remember my mother talking about it. There was something about Mrs. McAllister's mother being sick and that Carolyn had to take care of her. Her family was from somewhere in the East I think. I don't remember where."

"Did she have the baby there?"

"I . . . I guess so. All that I can remember is that she went away and when she came back she brought Kim with her."

"Let me see the other pictures."

Marty handed them to her.

Their lunch came but Eden pushed hers aside with her untouched drink and turned her attention to the photographs that had been taken that long-ago summer when she'd been sixteen.

She felt as though the world had stopped turning. As though everything, everyone in it had taken a deep breath and held it. Time stood still. The only sound left was the beating of her own heart.

Why hadn't she seen it? Why hadn't she known from the very beginning? She and Kim had laughed together when they'd put pepper on their popcorn or asked for burned bacon. They'd compared toes. Their eyes were practically the same, though Eden's were a shade darker. And they both had the same color hair. Was it only coincidence? A strange twist of fate that they looked so much alike?

She looked across the table at Marty and saw the same doubt, the same confusion in Marty's eyes.

She tried to tell herself it couldn't be true. Kim would have known if she'd been adopted. Everyone today told children when they were adopted. Linc would have told her if Kim had been her child.

He wouldn't have kept it from her; he wouldn't have lied to her.

She picked up the photographs and put them back in the manila envelope. "Can I keep these?" she asked.

"Of course, Eden, but—"

"Marty, I'm sorry, but I can't stay here." Eden put some money down on the table and pushed her chair back.

"I'll come with you," Marty said.

"No." Eden shook her head. "But I'll...I'll call you."

"Eden, are you...are you all right?"

"I don't know." Eden took a ragged breath. "I honestly don't know."

It took her five minutes to drive to Carter Prentice's office. His secretary said, "Mr. Prentice has been awfully busy this morning, Miss Adair. He's just getting ready to go to lunch."

"Tell him I'm here." Eden tightened her hands around her purse. "Tell him I have to see him."

"Well, I—"

"Tell him."

The young woman picked up the phone. "Miss Adair is here," she said into the receiver. "She insists on seeing you."

She listened, then nodded to Eden. "You can go in," she said crossly.

Mr. Prentice rose to greet her. "I've been trying to get you all morning," he said.

"You've opened the file?"

"Yes, Miss Adair. I have it here." His expression was troubled. "I've just finished reading it. I don't know what I expected, but . . ." He cleared his throat. "Perhaps you'd better sit down."

Eden sank into the chair across the desk from him. Her hands began to shake.

"Would you like a cup of tea?" he asked. "A glass of water?"

"No, thank you."

He picked a dark blue plastic folder up off the desk. "Would you like me to leave you alone for a few minutes?"

Eden took a deep breath. "Yes, thank you. Yes, I would."

He nodded. "I'll be outside if you need anything." He handed the file to her.

The door closed. Eden rubbed her hand over the blue plastic cover. Gold lettering on the front showed the date: March 2, 1976.

She closed her eyes. Remembered prayers echoed in her mind.

She opened the file. There was a birth certificate. "Baby girl Adair born March 2, 1976. Mother, Eden Adair, age seventeen. Father unknown."

And an adoption paper that read: "Baby girl Adair, adopted on March 4, 1976 by Dr. Lincoln McAllister and

Mrs. Carolyn McAllister, 425 Briarwood, Wiggins Bay, Florida.''

Eden stared blindly at the words that converged and faded and focused again.

''. . . adopted . . . by Dr. Lincoln McAllister and Carolyn McAllister.''

The room swayed, tilted. She grabbed the arms of the straight-backed chair and by the sheer force of her will she did not faint. Deep breaths, she told herself. Take deep breaths. Mr. Prentice will never be the same if he finds you stretched out on his floor.

Oh my God. My God!

Thoughts skittered round and round in her head like dead leaves blown by the wind.

Kim was her daughter.

Linc had lied to her.

He had told her he loved her. He had made love with her.

He had lied to her.

He had taken her baby. He and Carolyn. Nervous, nutsy-fruitsy Carolyn. Carolyn who had hit her young daughter with a ruler across the backs of her hands. Carolyn who had broken her daughter's finger. She had taken her daughter. She had taken her baby.

Linc had lied to her.

At last Eden gathered the file up and crossed the room to open the door.

Carter Prentice got up from where he'd been sitting in the outer office. ''Are you all right?'' he asked.

''Yes, I'm all right.'' She turned to his secretary. ''I wonder if you would be good enough to make me a copy of this?'' she said.

''Of course, Miss Adair. The copy machine's in the other room.''

"I realize this has come as a shock," Mr. Prentice said.

Eden nodded, but she didn't speak. She couldn't speak.

The secretary returned. She handed Eden a copy of the court transcript and asked if there was anything else she could do.

"No, thank you." Eden's mouth tightened. "I'll take care of everything now," she said.

Eden spent the rest of the afternoon in her room looking through Marty's envelope of photographs.

She should have known. The first time she had seen Kim she should have known she was her daughter. No wonder Linc had been upset when she and Kim started spending time together. No wonder he'd told her he didn't want her to see Kim again. From that very first day in his office when she told him she had come back to try to find her daughter, he had warned her to leave it alone.

She picked up a picture of herself with Dave Fenwell. "I hope they send him to prison for fifty years," Kim had said, not knowing she had been talking about the man who fathered her.

Kim mustn't know. She must never find out about Dave. She would tell her the truth about herself, about being her real mother, but she would never tell her about Dave.

Linc called her. He said, "Hi. How was your day?"

Fury curled like a red hot fire deep in the pit of Eden's stomach. She tightened her hand around the phone. "Interesting," she said.

"I can get away at six. Kim has plans so we'll have dinner alone. Any place special you'd like to go?"

"The boat. I'll meet you at the boat."

"Great idea. I'll pick up something. What'll it be? Chicken? Chinese? Or maybe pizza."

"I don't give a damn," she said.

"Eden? What's the matter?" He sounded concerned. "Are you all right?"

"No, I'm not all right."

For a moment there was silence on the other end of the phone. "What is it?" he asked.

"Later," she said. "I'll tell you later."

Eden left the house at five-thirty. She walked up and down the marina, her anger building with every step she took.

He came at ten minutes after six. There was concern in his eyes, a worry line between his brows.

"Sorry I'm late," he said. He reached out his hand for her but she ignored it and strode along the dock toward the boat.

"What in the hell is the matter?" He caught up with her and matched his stride to hers.

She kept on walking. When they got to the boat he tried to take her hand to help her aboard but she jumped onto the boat unaided.

"All right," he said. "Let's have it. What's going on?"

Eden opened her purse and handed him the picture that Marty had given her.

He looked at it, puzzled. "Good picture," he said. "Kim always squints into the sun like that."

"It isn't Kim," Eden said. "It's a picture of me."

Linc's face went white. He stared at her. He turned the picture over and saw the date.

"Eden," he said. "Eden, I—"

"Marty gave it to me at lunch." Her voice was so choked with anger she could barely speak. "I thought the same thing you did, that it was a picture of Kim. But it was me, Linc. Me when I was sixteen."

She clenched her hands tight to her sides to try to stop them from shaking. "I went to see Carter Prentice. He had the adoption file. I know, Linc. I know that Kim is my daughter." She fought to control the tears that spilled from her eyes. "Why didn't you tell me? How could you have let me see her, care for her, love her, and not tell me. You took my baby. You—"

"You gave her away." His voice, harsh in the silence of the night, was as tortured as hers.

Something gave way inside Eden. She gasped as the pain tore through her, she bent into it, moaned aloud with the force of it. But when he reached for her she backed away.

"I didn't have any choice," she whispered. "I was still in school. I couldn't go home. My father wouldn't have let me."

She swiped at her tears, angry because she was crying in front of him. "You made love to me," she whispered. "You pretended to care, Linc, but it was a lie. Everything you said, everything you did."

"Eden, please." He saw her pain, her anguish, but he couldn't help her. She knew. Oh my God, she knew about Kim.

A boat sped by and the *Kimmer* rocked. Eden grasped the back of a bolted-down deck chair to steady herself. "Why didn't you tell Kim that she was adopted?" She asked. "Why did you lie to her? Why didn't you tell her the truth?"

"Carolyn didn't want me to." Linc ran a hand across his face. He saw the anger in Eden's eyes and the disbelief. "She'd been adopted and when her adoptive parents had other children, they treated her differently. I knew it was wrong, Eden. I knew we should have told Kim, but I let Carolyn have her way. I shouldn't have.''

He took a deep breath of sea air and tried to clear his thoughts. ''Look,'' he said, ''we need to calm down. Let's go below and have a cup of coffee and talk about this.''

''I don't want to calm down,'' Eden said angrily. ''I don't want any coffee.''

''Then sit down.''

She clung to the back of her chair. ''Why?'' she asked. ''Why Kim? Why *my* baby?''

He braced himself against her anger and her pain. ''Carolyn . . . Carolyn and I . . . had been trying to adopt a baby for almost two years with the same agency that you talked to. She came into the office one day when you were there. She found out you weren't keeping your child and she said she wanted it.''

He faced Eden. ''I didn't, Eden. I tried to fight her. But when I delivered Kim . . .'' His voice shook when he remembered how close it had been, how hard he had fought to save the baby. ''We did it together, you and I. We brought her into the world and in a strange way that made her a part of both of us. That night, when I went to your room, when I held you and knew that it was tearing you apart to let your baby go, I felt a bonding with you. I told you the other night that I began to fall in love with you that night, Eden, and it's true. It was crazy. You were a kid. I was ten years older than you were and I was married.

''I went along with Carolyn,'' he said. ''I agreed to the adoption. And I loved Kim, Eden. Maybe somewhere in the back of my mind I knew that Dave Fenwell was her biological father but I wouldn't let myself think about it.

Kim was my child." He turned and looked at her. "Yours and mine, Eden."

"No," she said bitterly. "Not yours and mine. Yours and Carolyn's."

"We took care of her. We nursed her through her childhood sicknesses, we—"

"Carolyn hit her. She broke her finger. She was sick and neurotic. She—"

"She did the best she could," Linc said.

"With my child. *My* child."

"No!" he said harshly. "You gave her up. She wasn't yours."

"How could you, Linc? How could you!" She was crying hard now, hot bitter tears that blinded her eyes and ran down her cheeks. "It wasn't enough that you lied to Kim, you lied to me." Her voice broke. "You let me think there was something special between us, Linc. Something wonderful. Something—"

"There was," he said. "There is."

Eden shook her head. "Whatever it was…it was only make-believe. You were pretending. You—"

"No! What was…what is between us is real, Eden. Everything I said to you, the way I feel about you, that's real."

She sank down in the deck chair and covered her face with her hands. She thought of the words they had whispered in the darkness of the night, of the way they had touched each other, loved each other. But it had all been a lie. From the very beginning it had all been a lie.

"When I came back," she said, "when I went to your office that day to ask you to help me…" She brushed the tears away. "Why did you want to see me again? Why did you kiss me? Why did you . . ." She shook her head, unable to go on.

Linc took a step toward her. "Because I couldn't stay away from you," he said hoarsely. "I was terrified you'd find out the truth, Eden, but I couldn't stay away. For sixteen years Kim has been the most important person in my life. She's been my joy from the day she was born. She's brightened my life, she's made everything worthwhile. Then you came. I tried not to see you. I honestly tried. But I couldn't... I couldn't stay away from you."

He put both hands on the arms of the deck chair, imprisoning her there. "You can't tell her," he said.

"She's my daughter. I have the right."

"No!"

Eden tried to get up but he held her there.

"Kim loves me," she said desperately. "She said she wished I were her mother. Well I am her mother. I'm going to tell her that I am."

She shoved Linc's hands away and stood up, but when she started past him he grabbed her shoulders. "Don't do this," he said.

"Let me go."

"Stop thinking about yourself. Think about Kim. Think about what this will do to her."

Eden faced him. "And to you? When she knows you've lied to her all these years. When she finds out that Carolyn wasn't her real mother, that you're not her real father."

He gripped her shoulders tighter. "Would you rather she know that Dave Fenwell is her father?" he asked quietly. "Do you want her to know that the woman she has grown to love is the mother who gave her away sixteen years ago?"

Eden swayed and would have fallen if he hadn't been holding her. She closed her eyes and took a deep breath to steady herself. "I hate you," she said. "Oh God, how I hate you."

Her eyes, like shards of bright green stone, burned into his, she had to curl her hands tight to her body to keep from striking out at him. She pulled away, and grasping the deck rail she jumped down onto the dock.

Linc sank into the chair where she'd been sitting and put his head in his hands. "What am I going to do?" he said aloud. "What in the hell am I going to do?"

Chapter Fourteen

The next few days passed in a confusion of doubt and pain. Eden couldn't eat, she couldn't sleep. She stayed in her room and paced back and forth. When Kim called she said she had a cold.

"Have you seen Dad?" Kim asked anxiously. "Maybe he can give you an antibiotic of something."

"I'll be all right in a day or two."

"I wish you would have stayed with us. I loved having you there, Eden. It was so nice, kind of taking care of you, having breakfast with you. You know?"

"I know, Kimmy." Eden clamped down hard on her lower lip. She wanted to say, it can be like that always. We can be together because we belong together. You're my daughter. I love you and I want to be with you.

But everything had to be exactly right when she told Kim, when she said, "I'm your mother and I love you."

She tried not to think of Linc, of how he must be feeling.

Marty called. "You okay?" she asked.

"I'm not sure."

"I haven't told anybody," Marty said. "Not even Charlie. About the pictures, I mean."

Eden heard a match being struck and knew that Marty, who had quit smoking at least two dozen times, had started again. "It isn't a coincidence, is it, Eden?" Marty said. "I mean about you and Kim looking so much alike."

"No, Marty, it isn't a coincidence."

"Then she's your daughter. What...what are you going to do, Eden?"

"I don't know." Her hands started to shake again. "I want to tell her, Marty. I have the right..." She started to cry. "I want my baby back," she said.

"Eden...honey, take it easy. Do you want me to come over?"

"No, I... Thanks, Marty, but I think I just want to be alone for a little while."

"I'm here if you want me, Eden."

"I know, and thanks. I'll remember that."

She sat on the edge of her bed and planned how she would tell Kim. Do you remember when you said you wished I were your mother? she would say. Sometimes wishes come true, Kim. I really am your mother.

And she'd tell Kim how she'd held her for that one brief moment. She'd tell her... What? That she'd given her up a few hours after her birth? That the father she loved wasn't really her father? That he had lied to her? That she had been adopted?

Like Emily what's-her-name.

Kim had said that she felt sorry for Emily, that it was terrible for Emily to know that her mother hadn't wanted her, that she'd just given her away.

What if Kim asked who her real father was? What if she found out it was Dave Fenwell? What if she knew that she had been conceived because her mother had been raped?

Hour after hour Eden paced up and down in her room. Phoebe Rose, who knew that Eden was upset but didn't know why, came to the door four or five times each day. "You've got to eat," she said. "You're going to make yourself sick if you don't."

To please her, Eden would accept a sandwich or a salad. But she was never able to eat more than a bite or two.

Kim called every day. "Are you sure you're all right?" she asked again and again. "Are you sure you don't want to come over?"

Once she asked if Eden had seen Linc. "Has he called?" she wanted to know. "Have you seen him?"

And when Eden said no, Kim said, "Something's wrong, isn't it? Between you and Dad I mean. I'll talk to him, Eden. I'll—"

"No," Eden said. "Let it alone for now, Kim. Please just . . . let it alone."

On the afternoon of the fourth day that Eden had secluded herself in her room, Kim called again. "Elaine and I are going to go shopping in Ft. Myers," she said. "She's borrowed her dad's new car and wants to try it out. Why don't you come with us, Eden?"

"I don't think so, Kim. But thank you for asking."

"I'm coming over tomorrow," Kim said. "Cold or no cold, Eden, I'm coming over."

"Kim—"

"Gotta run. Elaine's waiting. See you tomorrow."

Tomorrow, Eden thought when she put down the phone. I'll tell her tomorrow.

She went downstairs for dinner that night and managed to eat half a bowl of chicken soup and part of a green salad. When the phone rang she said, "I don't want to talk to anybody."

Phoebe Rose went to answer it. From the kitchen Eden heard her say, "What? What's that? Oh Lord." Then Phoebe Rose called out, "It's Dr. Linc, Miss Eden."

"I don't want to talk to him."

Phoebe Rose came to the kitchen door. "It's...it's his daughter," she whispered. "There's been an accident."

Eden stared at her. With a cry she pushed her chair back and ran into the kitchen and grabbed the phone. "Linc? What is it?" she cried. "What's happened?"

"It's Kim." She heard the fear in his voice. "She and Elaine were driving back from Ft. Myers. Elaine tried to pass a truck. She lost control of the car. It...it went off the side of the road. It rolled over..."

Eden grasped the edge of the kitchen counter. "Where are you?"

"At the hospital. I've got to get back to her. I thought you should know."

She reached out a hand to Phoebe Rose. "How bad is it?"

"Bad."

Eden closed her eyes. "I'll be there in ten minutes." She put the phone down. "I've got to get to the hospital," she said.

Phoebe Rose took off her apron. "I'm coming with you."

Eden barely remembered the trip to the hospital. She drove blindly, automatically, hands so tight on the wheel that her knuckles were white.

At the emergency entrance parking lot she switched off the motor, and with Phoebe Rose beside her she ran toward the door.

"Dr. McAllister called me," she said to the nurse on duty. "His daughter has been in an accident."

"Yes, ma'am." The woman's face was solemn, sad. "Third floor," she said. "Ask for him at the nurse's station."

Eden hurried for the elevator with Phoebe Rose only a few steps behind her.

"Easy, Miss Eden," she said. "Dr. Linc's a good doctor. This is a wonderful hospital. Miss Kim's in good hands."

Eden nodded but she didn't try to answer. She was sick with fear, her stomach tight, her chest so constricted she could barely breathe.

They got off the elevator. She saw the nurse's station and when she reached it she said, "I'm Eden Adair. Dr. McAllister called me."

The nurse, a gray-haired woman in her mid-fifties looked up from the chart she'd been checking. "It's Room 305, Miss Adair. Dr. McAllister said you were to go right in when you came."

Phoebe Rose took Eden's hand.

Please, Eden prayed. Oh, please, let her be all right.

They went down the hall and passed a waiting room without glancing in.

"Miss Adair?" Eden turned when she heard her name. A girl with her arm in a sling got up and hurried toward her. It was Elaine. The teen's chin trembled and she started to cry. "It was my fault," she wept. "I shouldn't have tried to pass that truck. I . . ." She covered her face with her good hand.

An older man got up and put his arm around her. "I'm Elaine's father," he said. "I'm so sorry about this."

Eden couldn't speak. It was all she could do to keep from striking the weeping girl.

"We know you are." Phoebe Rose patted Elaine's shoulder. "Soon's we know something I'll come out and sit with you for a spell." She put her arm around Eden. "Come on now," she said. "Come on."

The door to 305 was closed. Eden tapped softly and opened it.

Linc stood on one side of Kim's bed. A nurse and a young man in a doctor's coat were on the other side. Kim's eyes were closed. She had a bandage around her head. There were scratches on her cheek and one eye was swollen shut. Her right leg had been propped up.

"Linc?"

He turned. His face was as white as the bandage around Kim's head.

"How is she?" Eden tried to keep her voice steady. "Tell me," she said.

"She has a head injury . . . bone fragments . . . and her leg is pretty badly banged up. She's been prepped for surgery. They'll be taking her up in a couple of minutes."

"Surgery?" Eden tried to swallow her fear. "Will you do it?"

Linc shook his head. He nodded toward the young man on the other side of the bed. "Clay, this is Miss Adair. Clay Contney, Eden. He'll do the surgery."

He was too young to be a doctor. Of medium height, blond and blue-eyed, he looked more like a college freshman than a surgeon.

"Dr. Contney's a neurosurgeon," Linc said. "One of the best. I called him a couple of hours ago and he flew in from Miami."

"I'm not as young as I look," Contney said.

Eden didn't believe him. She went closer to the bed and took one of Kim's hands in hers. "Kimmy," she whispered. "Kimmy?"

"She's been unconscious ever since they brought her in." Linc moved closer and stood beside her.

Two orderlies came in with a gurney. "We're ready for her, Doctor," one of them said.

"I'm going to scrub up." Contney rested a hand on Linc's shoulder. "Dr. Storer's standing by. He'll do her leg."

"Jim Storer's a good man," Linc said. "I'll observe in O.R."

Contney nodded. "I'll do everything I can," he said.

"I know." Linc's jaw clenched; his eyes were tortured.

They put Kim on the gurney. Eden didn't want to let go of her hand. "Let me go with her," she begged. "I want her to know that I'm with her. Just to the operating room, Linc. Please..."

He put an arm around her shoulders. "Take it easy," he said.

"She looks so small." Eden began to weep. "She's so pale. So..."

He motioned to Phoebe Rose. "I'll let you know as soon as it's over, but it's going to be two or three hours at least. You can wait here if you want to or out in the waiting room."

He let Eden go. "If you know any prayers..." He shook his head, then turned and hurried out of the room.

She prayed them all, silently, over and over again, word flowing into word. Don't let her die. Let her be all right. I'll promise anything, do anything. I'll never ask for anything again. She's only a girl. She hasn't even lived. She hasn't fallen in love, or married, or had babies of her own. She's my baby. Oh, please...

"Would you like some coffee, Miss Eden?" Phoebe Rose asked.

"No, thanks."

"Why don't we go out and sit in the waiting room for a little while? Kim's friend and her daddy are there. We could all be together, maybe help each other."

"I don't want to see her," Eden said. "It was her fault."

"She's only a girl, Miss Eden. I reckon she's suffering, too."

At last, though she didn't want to, Eden went out to the waiting room with Phoebe Rose.

Elaine was sitting close to her father. When she saw Eden she started to cry again. Eden sat down beside her. "Don't cry," she said.

"I was going too fast." Elaine raised a tearstained face. "I was so excited by my dad's new car. I... I wanted to show Kim how fast it would go. I thought I could pass that truck. I thought..." She put her hands up over her face and began to sob.

Eden put her arms around her. "Maybe you'd better take her home," she said to Elaine's father.

"She doesn't want to leave. Her mother's in Cleveland. I called her. She'll be in tonight." He shook his head. "I'm so sorry about this," he said. "I know how awful it must be for Dr. McAllister. Are you a relative?"

"No," Eden said. "No, I'm just... just a family friend."

* * *

Two hours went by. Three. Eden paced the corridor. She left the waiting room and went into Kim's room and then to the nurses' station. There wasn't any word yet, the gray-haired nurse told her.

"I'll tell you as soon as there is," she said. "Try not to worry. Dr. Contney is a wonderful surgeon."

Elaine fell asleep against her father's shoulder. Phoebe Rose went down to the coffee shop for coffee and sandwiches. They drank the coffee but the sandwiches went untouched.

Four hours went by. Elaine's father finally took Elaine home. Eden stood at the window and looked at the lights of the city below. People would be watching the late news now. They'd make comments about what was happening in Beirut or the West Bank and they'd look worried or pleased about what had happened to the Dow Jones that day. They wouldn't know that a girl's life depended on the skill of a surgeon who looked like a college freshman.

A few minutes after midnight a nurse that Eden hadn't seen before came to the door of the waiting room. "The surgery's over," she said. "Dr. McAllister is on his way down."

Eden reached for Phoebe Rose's hand.

His face was tired and lined. He was wearing surgical greens, the mask still hanging around his neck.

"Kim came through the surgery," he said. "She's in intensive care. It looks..." He sucked air into his lungs. "It looks pretty good."

Eden tried to stand up but her legs buckled and she sank back down to the chair. "Can I see her?" she whispered. "Please, Linc. Let me see her."

"She's not conscious, but..." He hesitated. "Yes," he said, "you can see her."

Phoebe Rose put her arm around Eden, but she waited outside when Eden and Linc went into the intensive care unit.

There were tubes in Kim's nose and in her arms. She was on a respirator. Her head was swathed in bandages and her right leg was elevated.

Eden, careful of the needle in Kim's wrist, stroked the pale hand. "Hi, Kimmy," she whispered. "Hi, sweetheart. I'm here, Kim. I'm here, baby."

Linc bit down hard on the inside of his cheek. He'd never tell her how close it had been or that once Jim Storer had said, "We're losing her."

"The hell we are!" Clay Contney had retorted. "Come on, Kimbo," he'd said. "Come on, dammit!" And when she'd rallied, his eyes had met Linc's. "She's going to make it," he'd murmured. "By God, she's going to make it."

And she had. But the next forty-eight hours would be touch and go.

A nurse stepped up to Kim's bed. She checked the IV. "I'll be on duty all night, Dr. McAllister," she said. "I'll keep a close watch on her."

"Thank you, Aileen." He put his arm around Eden's shoulders. "We have to go now," he said. "We can come back later."

"I don't want to leave her."

"The nurse will be here, Eden." He exerted enough pressure to turn her away from the bed.

When the door of intensive care closed behind them she leaned against the wall and closed her eyes.

"You'd better go home and try to get some sleep," Linc said.

Eden shook her head. "Not until I know she's out of danger."

"It may be a couple of days, Eden. Why don't you let me drive you and Phoebe Rose home?"

"No, I want to stay."

"All right, we'll stay together."

For the first time since she'd arrived at the hospital, Eden really looked at him. She'd been so preoccupied with her own worry, her own fear, that she'd been almost unaware of how he must be feeling. "You need a cup of coffee," she said.

"Yeah, I guess I do. I—" He saw Clay Contney coming down the corridor and without realizing it he reached for Eden's hand. "I...I thought you'd gone back to Miami," he said when the young doctor reached them.

"Nope." Contney nodded a hello to Eden. "Going to check on my girl. Why don't you and your lady go home, Doctor? I'll hang around here for a while."

"No," Linc said. "We'll stay. We'll be in the I.C. waiting room. Stop in after you've seen Kim."

"Will do."

Eden shook her head when Contney disappeared through the swinging doors. "He looks like such a kid," she said.

"He's twenty-eight. Head of his class at Harvard Medical. Did his residency at Boston Mass, and he's a top neurosurgeon at Jackson."

"He still looks like a kid to me."

The shadow of a smile tugged at Linc's mouth. "Come on," he said. "Let's put Phoebe Rose in a taxi."

Phoebe Rose didn't want to leave, but Eden insisted. "I'll call you if there's any change," she said.

Phoebe Rose hugged her, then Linc went downstairs with her and put her in a cab. When he came back, Clay Contney was in the waiting room with Eden.

"Kim's doing as well as can be expected," he reported to Linc.

A muscle jumped in Linc's cheek. "You did a nice piece of work, Clay. I'm grateful. Will I see you in the morning or do you have to get back to Miami?"

Clay stretched his long legs out in front of him. "I'm going to stick around, at least for tomorrow."

Eden glanced at Linc. He saw the fear in her eyes. "That's good of you, Clay," he said. "I appreciate it."

The hour grew late. Every thirty minutes both Clay and Linc went in to check on Kim and each time they came back Linc said, "There's been no change, Eden."

At three in the morning Clay checked on Kim one more time. When he came out he said, "I'm going to sack out for a little while. I've left word to call me if there's any change." He rested a hand on Linc's shoulder. "She's going to make it," he said.

When they were alone Eden leaned her head back against the green vinyl chair. "Maybe you'd better try to get some rest, too, Linc. If you've got office hours tomorrow—"

"McCluskey will cover for me." He looked at her. "Why don't you stretch out on the couch for a while, Eden?"

She shook her head and said, "I'm all right."

But she wasn't all right. Her face was pale and pinched and her hands were shaking. He thought about the argument they'd had on the boat and it seemed to him as though it had happened a long time ago. He wouldn't think about that now. All that mattered was that Kim would recover. He would deal with the rest of it later.

By morning her vital signs had improved and she was taken off the respirator. But she still hadn't regained consciousness.

Linc drove Eden home and left instructions with Phoebe Rose that she was to go to bed. But when he went back to the hospital a few hours later Eden was there, pacing the hall in front of I.C.U.

They went in together to see Kim.

"She's doing better," Clay said when he looked up and saw them. "What we've got to do now is hope and pray that she regains consciousness soon." He moved away so that Eden could sit down.

She took Kim's hand in hers and kissed it. "Hi, Kimmy," she said. "It's Eden, darling. Your dad and I are here, sweetheart."

Kim's lips moved. She wet her lips with her tongue. "Mama?" she whispered. "Mama?"

"Yes, darling," Eden said. "Mama's here, Kim."

Linc turned away and gripped the end of the bed. Tears formed and fell and he knew that for as long as he lived he would never forget this moment, or the sound of Eden's voice when she said, "Mama's here, Kim."

The next afternoon Kim was moved into a private room. She still floated in and out of consciousness but all of her vital signs were good.

Eden sat on the side of her bed for hours. She held Kim's hand and talked to her. She told her all about growing up in Michigan, about her childhood friends there. She told her about the summer she'd spent in Wiggins Bay, about her friend Marty, and what it had been like to swim in the Gulf of Mexico for the very first time.

"Lake Michigan is so cold," she said. "Even in the summer it's like somebody dropped ice cubes into the lake. I used to get goose bumps when I was a little girl and I still do when I swim there now. But the Gulf isn't like that, is it, Kim? It's almost like stepping into a luke-warm bath and I love it."

She stroked Kim's forehead. "We'll swim a lot when you're better, Kim. We'll take a lunch and picnic on the beach. We'll go to Sanibel and hunt for seashells."

She told funny stories about her Aunt Jo, about the poker parties and her aunt's old fishing buddies. She talked and talked and on the fifth day after the accident Kim opened her eyes and said, "Hi. Hi, Eden."

"Hi, baby," Eden said just as Linc came into the room. "Your dad's here, honey."

"Daddy?"

Linc took the chair beside the bed. "How're you doing, Kimmer?" he asked.

"Okay, I guess." Kim looked around the room. "What am I doing here?"

"There was an accident, Kim. You were pretty badly hurt."

"An accident?" Her eyes widened and she flinched. "Elaine?" she said. "Is Elaine all right?"

"Her arm was broken, but yes, she's all right."

Kim reached for Eden's hand. "I'm glad you're here," she said. "Don't leave. Okay?"

"I won't."

Kim yawned. "I think I want to sleep now. My head hurts."

"It will be better soon," Linc said.

"Promise, Daddy?"

"I promise, Kimmer."

Eden looked at him. "She's going to be all right now, isn't she?"

So filled with thanksgiving that he could barely speak, Linc covered Eden's hand with his. "Yes," he said. "She's going to be all right."

But Eden wouldn't leave. "I have to be here when she wakes up," she insisted. "I told her I'd be here."

He had a lounge chair moved into the room and every day Phoebe Rose brought Eden a change of clothes and something to eat.

By the end of the week Kim's headaches had stopped and she was able to sit up.

Jim Storer came every day. "Her leg is coming along," he said, "but she'll have to have a lot of therapy. I'd say that by Christmas she'll be almost back to normal."

Clay Contney had returned to Miami, but he flew in every second or third day.

"He's so swass," Kim told Eden. "For an older man I mean."

The next time he was due she asked Eden to brush her hair and loan her a lipstick. A small bandage was still wrapped around her head, but Eden brushed around it, then dug in her purse for a pale coral lipstick.

And when Clay Contney came in he said, "Excuse me, I'm looking for Kim McAllister. Short girl with blond hair and green eyes..." He gave an exaggerated gasp. "Good heavens, is it...could it be...is it really you?"

Kim giggled. It was the most wonderful sound Eden had ever heard.

"How's the old noggin today?" he asked Kim.

"Fine. When can I get the bandage off?"

"How about right now?" He reached for a pair of bandage scissors. "We had to cut some of your hair," he told her when he began to unwrap the bandage, "but just in one spot. I think you can probably comb over it until it grows back.''

He finished unwrapping, but before he handed Kim a mirror, he very gently rearranged her hair to cover the bare spot and the scar.

She examined herself critically in the mirror and said, ''I look pretty good.''

''Pretty good? You look stupendous, Kimbo.''

She blushed. ''Dad said you were a wonderful surgeon, Dr. Contney.'' She held her hand out to him. ''Thank you for taking such good care of me. I'm very grateful.''

Clay took her hand and a strange expression crossed his face. ''You helped, too, Kim. I knew you were fighting right along with me. I knew that together we'd make it.''

''Together,'' Kim said.

And Eden, watching, knew that Kim wasn't a little girl anymore. In some mysterious way, a way that she could not define, Kim had become a young woman.

Chapter Fifteen

A week later Linc and Eden took Kim home.

"You're coming with us, aren't you?" Kim had asked when it was time to leave the hospital.

Before Eden could answer Linc had said, "Of course she is."

For over a week and a half Eden had barely left Kim's side. She had been with her night and day, speaking softly, soothingly whenever Kim stirred. As much as Kim needed her, Eden needed Kim. He didn't know what was going to happen later, whether or not Eden would, as she had said, tell Kim that she was her mother. But he would face that when it came. For now it was enough that Kim wanted Eden with her and that Eden was here.

At the house Kim insisted Eden take the room next to hers. "It was my mother's room," she said when she and Eden were alone. "She and Dad had separate rooms for just about as long as I remember. I suppose it was because she wasn't well a lot of the time, and probably because sometimes Dad got emergency calls in the middle of the night. She said he disturbed her rest.''

Kim shifted on her pillows so that she could look out of the window. ''It's a pretty room, Eden, with the same view of the garden that I have. Mother liked that. She'd sit in her chair by the window for hours, looking out into the garden, or reading. She liked to read, poetry mostly. Sometimes I'd go into her room and she'd read to me. I didn't always understand the poetry but I loved the rhythm of the words and the sound of her voice.''

Everything in Carolyn's room, a delicate, fragile ladylike room, was pink and ivory. An ivory quilted bedspread covered the bed. An ivory-backed comb, brush and mirror set were neatly arranged on the dressing table in front of untouched perfume bottles.

This was the room of the woman who had raised her daughter. She hadn't been an unkind woman, but surely a self-absorbed, neurotic woman.

Linc's wife. He had lain with her here. He had tried to share his life with her, and for a little while he had loved her.

Eden wondered what it had been like for him, how it had been to come home night after night to a woman like Carolyn. Had he found solace elsewhere? Somehow Eden didn't think so. Besides, he'd had Kim. Most of the responsibility of raising her had been on his shoulders.

Linc's room, the master bedroom, was just across the hall from Kim's, and he kept his door ajar so that he would hear her if she needed him.

Eden's door was ajar, too, and night after night he heard her get up and tiptoe into Kim's room to make sure that Kim was all right. Sometimes he heard her whisper to Kim and he would lie there in the darkness of his room, touched by Eden's devotion, wishing with all his heart that after she had seen Kim she would return to his bed rather than her own.

Her bed that had once been Carolyn's bed.

How many times had he stood in the doorway of that room, longing for the comfort that only a woman who loved him could give?

How many times had he called her name and heard her answer, "I'm terribly tired, Linc. I had a really dreadful day"?

How many times? How many times?

Once in a while, with a martyred sigh, she had let him come into her room and allowed him to touch her. "But not my breasts," she always said. "I can't stand to have anybody touch my breasts."

I'm not anybody, he'd wanted to say. I'm your husband.

She had lain there, as though trying to be patient, her body rigid and unrelenting, doing what she had once referred to as her duty.

After a while he no longer imposed himself on her.

Making love to Eden hadn't been like that. She had been so willing, so eager in her response to him. She had welcomed him joyfully and when she'd lifted her body to his she'd whispered, "Yes, oh yes. I love that, yes."

It made him feel guilty that he compared the two women. Carolyn couldn't help being the way she had been.

And Eden couldn't help being who she was. Kim's mother, come back to claim her child.

He hired a nurse to take care of Kim, but after only two days Eden said, "I can take care of her, Linc. There really isn't any need for a nurse."

"She's going to need fairly constant care until her leg heals," he'd argued. "That's a lot of work, Eden. She can't stand alone, she can't get to the bathroom by herself. It's enough that you're here."

"No, it isn't. I want to do it, Linc." She looked at him, her eyes wide with appeal. "I've never really done anything for her. Please let me do this. I need to do it."

In the end he had given in.

It had been the same with the therapist, a capable but dour woman who came for an hour every day, five days a week.

"She looks like a fullback," Kim said. "She's so rough, Dad, and she never smiles. It hurts a lot to move my leg the way she wants me to. I wouldn't mind because I know that I have to do the movements in order to get my leg back to the way it was, but she's so unpleasant about it. She *orders* me to do the movements instead of asking me to."

"I've watched her," Eden said. "The exercises are fairly simple, Linc. I can do the same thing she does and I don't look like a fullback."

You sure as hell don't, Linc thought.

So in addition to taking over the duties of the nurse, Eden became Kim's therapist. She asked, she cajoled, she kibitzed, but she never ordered.

"Ten more," she'd say. "Come on, Kim, you can do it. Do fifteen and I'll make a batch of brownies for dinner."

"You make terrible brownies," Kim would say. But she'd do the fifteen exercises because Eden had asked her to.

Mrs. Parkins, the housekeeper, came every morning at eight, but it was Eden who prepared Kim's breakfast and carried it upstairs.

"Hi, sunshine," she'd say. "How's my girl?"

And every time she said it Linc felt as though he'd received a blow to his solar plexus.

She's going to tell her, he thought. One of these days she's going to tell Kim the truth.

Clay Contney flew in once a week from Miami. He always said that there was a special case at the hospital he had to check on, and he always managed to come by the house on Briarwood. "To check on my star patient," he said.

One particularly balmy afternoon he came while Linc was still at his office, and because the day was sunny and bright he carried Kim down the stairs and into the garden.

He placed her carefully on one of the chaises and Kim smiled up at him. "It's so good to be outside," she said. "I love it here, Dr. Contney. Thank you for bringing me down."

"You're welcome, pussycat. But how about calling me Clay?"

"Clay." She blushed. "It's a good strong name. I like it."

"Can you stay for lunch?" Eden asked, and when Clay said that he could, she prepared a shrimp and crabmeat salad and served it outside under the trees.

Kim, who wore little white shorts and a green-and-white striped shirt, had never been prettier. And though Clay directed most of his conversation to Eden it seemed to Eden that whenever he turned to say something to Kim there was a subtle change in the timbre of his voice. His smile became more gentle and his eyes softened.

As for Kim, she smiled when he smiled, looked serious when he looked serious and laughed when he made

a joke. Like the first rose of spring she blossomed before Eden's eyes.

That night when Eden came in to tell her good-night
Kim patted the side of her bed and motioned Eden to sit
beside her. "Clay...Dr. Contney's awfully nice, isn't
he?"

"Yes, he is."

"Do you know how old he is?"

"I think your dad told me he was twenty-eight."

Kim nodded. "I'm almost seventeen," she said.

That night after she had tucked Kim in, Eden made a
cup of coffee and went to sit out in the garden so that
Linc could spend some time alone with his daughter. She
listened to the nightbirds coming to roost in the mango
trees. She remembered how it had been the night she and
Linc had made love here, how cool and fresh the grass
had felt beneath her back, how sweetly scented with
night-blooming jasmine the air had been.

When she had confronted Linc the night she had
learned that Kim was her daughter she had told him that
everything that had passed between them had been a lie.
But that wasn't true; the night they had made love here
hadn't been a lie. They had shared more than passion
that night; they had shared love. For as long as she lived
she would never forget the way it had been, or how in that
final soaring moment they had clung together, man and
woman joined by heart and by love.

They had been careful of each other these last few
weeks. All of their attention had been focused on Kim,
but sooner or later, Eden knew, they would have to talk.

She was just getting ready to go in when he came out
into the garden. "I saw the fresh pot of coffee on the

stove," he said. He indicated the cup in his hand. "I thought you might be out here."

"I was just going in."

"I wish you wouldn't. I wish we could talk for a little while."

Eden settled back into the chaise. "All right," she said. "As a matter of fact, there is something I've been wanting to talk to you about. School starts in two weeks but Kim won't be ready to go back for at least another month. I've written my school to ask for a leave of absence, Linc. I thought I could tutor Kim at home, if it's all right with you."

He hadn't thought about Kim's school, nor had he thought about Eden's leaving. She had become a part of his and Kim's lives these past few weeks; he didn't know what it would be like when she had gone.

"I'm not trying to take over," she said. "I know it must seem like that, Linc, I mean the way I've moved in on you. But Kim's better now and able to get around a little on her own. I'll move back into Aunt Jo's house at the end of the week."

He frowned. "Kim's gotten used to your being here," he said.

"I'll still come every day to do the therapy and tutor her. I'm qualified but if you'd rather have the school arrange for someone else I'll understand."

"No." Linc shook his head. "No, Eden, I'd rather have you tutor Kim."

He wanted to speak to her about what had happened that night on the boat. It had to be talked about and yet he was reluctant to bring it up. He had relived the scene over and over in his mind, and the picture of Eden, of the young Eden who had looked so much like Kim, had imprinted itself in his brain.

There had not been time these last few weeks, when their only concern had been for Kim, to talk about it. But sooner or later he and Eden would have to face what had happened that night. She had told him that she would tell Kim that she was her birth mother and he had told her she didn't have the right to do that, that she had lost whatever rights she had had when she gave her child up.

It needed to be talked about; he had to know what she was going to do.

He put his coffee cup down on the table between them. "You know how grateful I am for everything you've done for Kim," he said.

Eden looked at him.

"You've been here for her, Eden. You've been her mother in every sense of the word. I know how much she cares about you, how very much you mean to her." Linc hesitated. "Isn't that enough, Eden?" he asked. "Isn't it enough to know that she loves you and that you're a very important part of her life?"

"No," Eden said. "It isn't enough. I have to tell her. I know you think I'm wrong and I'm sorry. But I need her, Linc, and I think she needs me."

She faced him, hands clasped together. "I know you're afraid of what it will do to yours and Kim's relationship, but Kim loves you. Nothing I say could ever change the way she feels about you. She'll understand why you didn't tell her that she was adopted."

"Will she understand why you gave her away?"

Eden closed her eyes. Don't get angry, she told herself. Understand how hard this is for him, how afraid he is that it will change everything.

"I can only hope that she will," she said. "Kim has grown up since the accident. She's not a girl any longer, Linc. She's a young woman."

There was a strength and a firmness in her voice that hadn't been there that night on the boat when she had confronted him with the photograph.

"She's only sixteen," he said.

"She's going to be seventeen." And because she thought he should know, she said, "Kim has a crush on Clay."

Linc looked at her, not understanding. "Clay?" he said. "That's impossible."

A slight smile curved Eden's lips. "Is it?"

"He's old enough to be her father."

"He's twenty-eight."

"It's ridiculous."

"Probably. But I thought I should tell you."

"Well by God, I won't allow it. I'll speak to Clay, I'll tell him he'd damn well better stay away from her. I..."

We're like husband and wife, he thought. She's telling me about our daughter's crush on an older man and I'm being the outraged father, huffing and puffing and saying how ridiculous it is.

If they really were husband and wife they'd argue about it. Eden would calm him down. Maybe they'd chuckle about it, and maybe they'd feel a little sad because their daughter was growing up.

He would take her hand and in a little while they would go back to the house together, upstairs to their room together. He would hold her and they would make love, and finally they would sleep, spoon fashion, their bodies close and warm and touching.

If they were husband and wife.

"I'd better go up and check on Kim." Eden stood up. "Don't worry about Clay," she said. "He's a decent man. He'd never do anything to hurt Kim."

Linc nodded, glad of the darkness so that she could not see his face. "I think I'll sit here a little longer," he murmured.

Eden rested her hand on his shoulder. "Good night, Linc," she said.

He wanted to touch her. He wanted to say, don't go in. Stay here with me, talk to me. I love you, Eden. I need you.

Instead he said, "Good night, Eden. Sleep well."

Then he was alone in the quiet of the night, alone to think about the years ahead. The years without Eden.

She stood by the bedroom window looking down at him and it seemed to her that she could feel his pain, his uncertainty, and his unhappiness. She wanted to tell him that she understood, and that she loved him.

At last, because she could not help herself, she went back down the stairs and out into the garden, so quietly that he did not hear until she said, "Linc?"

He looked up. She saw the question and the pain in his dark cinnamon eyes.

"What is it?" he asked. "Is something wrong?"

"No, nothing's wrong." She touched the side of his face. "I'd like to be with you tonight," she said. "I need to be close to you, Linc. If you . . . if you want to."

His heart lurched because it was almost as though she had read his mind, as though a little while ago she had looked into his head and into his heart and had seen his need to hold her and to love her.

He brought her hand to his lips and held it there for a moment. He didn't know what the future held for them; he only knew that one thing was true and sure. He loved her.

They went into the house and upstairs to Kim's room. They stood beside her bed, looking down at her. "She's so beautiful," Eden whispered.

"Because she's yours," he said.

She leaned back against him and he put his arms around her waist. I wish it could always be like this, she thought. I wish we could be a family. That I could be with him, and with her, for the rest of my life. I would ask nothing more, only this, this perfect time with the two people I love most in the world.

They went into his bedroom and closed the door. They were alone, alone to hold each other. He kissed her with a hunger too long bottled up, with fever and passion and a need that he had never before known.

With eager hands they undressed each other, and stood for a little time, body pressed to body, close, touching, one with the other.

"There's so much I want to say to you," Eden said.

"I know."

But the emotions between them were too great for words tonight; they could only hold each other, warm and comfort each other.

He led her to his bed. In the shadowed light of the room he laid her down, but when she began to pull the sheet up to cover her nakedness he said, "No, I want to look at you."

He touched her with hands made gentle by love. He traced the lines and the planes of her body as though she were a precious jewel. He kissed her forehead and her cheeks, her lips, the palms of her hands, her fingertips, her shoulders and her breasts, not with hunger or with fierceness but with tenderness. With love.

He didn't know what tomorrow would bring or how they would resolve the terrible problem that divided them, but for this little while Eden was his. She belonged to him, as he belonged to her.

She knew by the way he touched and caressed her that tonight was different. Her heart cried out to him. Forgive me for what I have to do and love me. Oh, Linc, please love me.

Their bodies bonded in perfect bliss. They moved as one person, bone of bone and flesh of flesh. They whispered love words against each other's lips and rode the crest of passion together.

In that final moment something deep and wonderful stirred within Linc's breast and his heart quivered with a feeling he had never known.

"Ah, Eden," he said. He rained kisses on her face and held her while their bodies yearned and strained, and shuddered in a final and joyous release.

And when they lay replete and close he said, "Something happened just now. Something more I mean. Something wonderful."

"I know," she said. "I know."

Eden left him sometime during the night, and when he awoke in the morning he heard her downstairs in the kitchen. He lay for a few minutes, happier than he had been in a long time. His body was relaxed, his mind was clear. He knew at last what he was going to do.

Eden smiled when he came into the kitchen and when he put his arms around her she raised her face for his kiss. She looked fresh and beautiful this morning. Her eyes were a clear sea green and her lips were sweetly vulnerable.

He kissed her again and when he let her go he said, "Ask Phoebe Rose if she'll stay with Kim tonight. We're going to take the boat out."

"I don't like to leave her, Linc."

He put a finger under her chin. "We need some time, Eden, just you and me. I—"

The phone rang. He answered it, said, "Yes, just a moment," and handed it to her. "It's Mr. Prentice," he said.

Eden took the phone.

"Good morning, Miss Adair," Prentice said. "I've just learned that Dave Fenwell's trial is scheduled for the middle of next month. Mr. Samuel Ginsburg, the District Attorney, wants to talk to you. He'd like to go over your statement again and be sure that you still want to testify."

"I want to testify."

"You should be aware that it might be a little rough, Miss Adair."

"I can stand rough."

"Very well, then. I've set up an appointment for you with Mr. Ginsburg at three this afternoon."

"I'll be there." Eden looked at Linc when she put the phone down. "Dave's trial is next month," she said. "I'm not looking forward to it."

He rested his hands on her shoulders. "We'll face it together," he said. "Do you want me to go to the D.A.'s office with you today?"

Eden shook her head. "Thanks, Linc, but I can handle it."

He kissed her again. "If you're sure," he said. "But remember our date tonight. You and me time, Eden. Tonight on the boat."

Samuel Ginsburg, the District Attorney for Lee County, rose to greet Eden when his secretary ushered her into his office that afternoon.

A man of medium height, with a worry line between his bushy eyebrows, steel-gray eyes and a firm mouth, he was impeccably dressed in a lightweight three-piece suit.

He offered his hand and said, "Good of you to come, Miss Adair. This is an unpleasant business but we might as well get on with it."

He held a chair out and when he had seated her, and asked if she wanted coffee, he said, "I understand you knew Dave Fenwell a long time ago."

"I met Dave when I first came to Wiggins Bay almost seventeen years ago, Mr. Ginsburg. But I haven't lived here for a long time. I returned this past June because my aunt had died and I had to settle her estate."

"You and Fenwell dated when you were here before?"

"Yes, we did. But only for a few weeks."

"I see." He tapped his long, bony fingers on the top of his mahogany desk. "Did you continue to see him after he raped you?"

Eden gasped. "How . . . did you know?" she managed to say.

"Why didn't you report it?" he asked, ignoring her question. "Why didn't you notify the police?"

He had taken her so by surprise that it was a moment before she could regain her composure. "I was sixteen when it happened. I...I was a virgin, Mr. Ginsburg. I was too ashamed to tell anyone, even my aunt."

Eden looked down at her hands. "I don't see what this has to do with what occurred a few weeks ago. I don't see any reason to bring it up now."

"I do." He looked across his desk at her. "I intend to put Fenwell away for a long time, Miss Adair. And I can, with your help."

Eden shook her head. "I've brought a charge of assault and attempted rape against him," she said. "The past is past. I'm sure the Statute of Limitations has expired."

"Of course it has," he said impatiently. "He can't be prosecuted for what happened a long time ago but I can make damn sure that the jurors hear about it."

"No." Eden shook her head. "No," she said again. "If you do, if that's what you're going to do, I'll withdraw my charges. I won't testify against him."

Ginsburg's mouth drew together in a thin, hard line. "You can't do that," he said.

"I can and I will."

"The man raped you once and he tried again a few weeks ago." Ginsburg exploded in anger. "Don't you want him to pay for what he did?"

"Yes, I want him to pay and if I were the only one involved I'd say to hell with it and with him." Eden stood up. She put her hands flat on the desk and looked at him. "I won't let anyone else be hurt by this, even if it means that Dave Fenwell walks away a free man. I'll testify to what he tried to do to me six weeks ago, but if you attempt to bring up what happened in the past I'll walk out of the courtroom. That's not a threat, Mr. Ginsburg, it's a promise."

He glared at her. A muscle jumped in his cheek. He turned around and stared out of his window. "All right," he said when he turned back to her. "You're making a mistake but we'll do it your way."

"Thank you." Eden offered her hand. "I'll be moving back into my own house at the end of the week," she said. "You can reach me there."

"I understand you've been staying with Dr. McAllister and his daughter since her accident. I hope she's better."

"She is, thank you."

"I'll be in touch then. If you change your mind—"

"I won't," she said.

Chapter Sixteen

Eden took special care getting ready for her date with Linc that night. She bathed in scented water, and when she had dried herself and done her hair and her makeup she put on the pink-and-white skinny-strapped dress she'd worn the afternoon they'd taken the boat to Naples. Her only jewelry was the gold bracelet that Kim had given her and a pair of pink-and-white shell earrings.

Linc was waiting for her when she came down the stairs. Broad of shoulder and narrow of hip, he truly was one of the most handsome men she had ever seen. And she loved him.

He kissed her and took her hand, and together they went into the living room.

Kim was propped up on the sofa and Phoebe Rose sat in one of the easy chairs in front of the coffee table. They were watching *Casablanca* and both of them were crying.

"You've seen that movie at least twenty times." Linc stooped to kiss his daughter's cheek.

"I know." Kim sniffed and wiped her eyes. "You look beautiful," she told Eden. "You and Dad have a good time."

"Okay, cutie. See you later. We won't be late."

"Take your time," Phoebe Rose said. "We've got two Westerns and *The Man with Two Heads* after this."

"The Man With Two Heads?" Linc said when he and Eden were in the car. "You've got to be kidding. Poor Phoebe Rose'll never want to baby-sit Kim again."

"She isn't baby-sitting. She's only keeping Kim company." Eden smiled. "You forget that Kim is almost seventeen, Linc."

The same age you were when pregnant. He thought the words but didn't say them.

"Clay came by this afternoon," she said.

"What did he have to say?" Linc headed the car toward the beach.

"That Kim was in great shape and that he'd never seen eyes exactly that color before."

"That's good. He..." His head jerked around. "What?" he asked in a voice that was just a decimal below a roar. "What in the hell's going on?"

"Chemistry."

"Chemistry, hell! Kim's only a kid."

"A well-developed, beautiful kid with a definite case of hero worship."

"I can understand that, but what about Clay? He's years older than she is."

"Twelve years."

"Okay, dammit, twelve. But he should know better. Kim isn't even out of high school."

Eden sighed. "I know."

"You'd better keep an eye on her."

"I won't be here, Linc. I'm moving back in with Phoebe Rose the day after tomorrow. Kim's leg is healing quickly, she'll be able to go to school in about three weeks."

"What about you, Eden? About your school, I mean?"

"It depends."

On Kim, he thought with a tightening of his stomach. On what Kim does when Eden tells her. But he didn't want to talk about that, not tonight.

They walked hand in hand down the dock toward the boat. He tried not to think about the last time they'd been here, of the bitter quarrel, the angry words. She had said that she hated him that night.

He felt a twinge of doubt. Maybe he shouldn't have suggested the boat, maybe they should have gone to a restaurant instead. But he hadn't wanted the hustle and bustle of a crowded restaurant tonight. He and Eden needed to be alone.

He took her hand to help her aboard, and went to unfasten the tie lines.

"I thought we'd go up around Bonita Springs," he said when he maneuvered the *Kimmer* out of the harbor.

"It's going to be a lovely night." Eden looked back toward the town, then out at the blue-green water. "I love it here," she said. "I'm going to miss it."

She knew they had to talk about Kim, and about themselves, but for a little while she wanted to put all of the serious things aside and simply enjoy the night. And Linc.

Last night had been special in a way she couldn't explain. She and Linc had come together with the sweet familiarity of a man and a woman who have made love many times before. It had not been better than passion, but in a strange way it had been more. In giving each other the gift of love, their very souls had touched.

She had not thought it possible to love anyone the way she loved Linc. He was her other half; with him she became whole. He was the happiness she had been searching for all of her life.

She stood beside him when they headed toward Bonita. The air was cooler out here on the water and the offshore breeze was brisk and fresh. Linc unfurled the sails and the only sounds were of the sea, the cry of gulls, the splash of the fish. She took a deep breath and filled her lungs with the clean, salt-scented air. She leaned her face against his shoulder and wished that it could always be like this.

When they were a few miles off shore Linc dropped the anchor. The night was soft and filled with promise; the boat rocked gently on the incoming tide.

"I thought we'd have champagne, if that's all right with you," he said.

"Yes, of course. I love champagne." Eden smiled up at him. "We're being a little festive, aren't we?"

"A little," he said.

He went below and returned with a silver ice bucket with a bottle of champagne cooling in it and two fluted crystal glasses.

"Elegant," Eden said, "or as Kim would say, *très* cool."

"*Très,*" he said.

He poured champagne into each of their glasses and touched his glass to hers. "To you," he said.

"And to you, Linc."

"How did it go today? What did you think of Sam Ginsburg?"

"I think he's a capable professional but I'm not sure I like him."

Linc chuckled. "Sam isn't a lovable man, but you're right, he is capable. If anybody can put Dave Fenwell away for a few years Sam can."

"He knew about the rape," she said. "I don't know how he knew, Linc. Maybe Dave bragged to some of his friends about what he did, or maybe Mr. Fenwell told his cronies." Eden took a sip of her champagne. "Ginsburg wanted to bring the rape up in court. I told him that if he did I'd drop the charges against Dave and that I'd refuse to testify."

She tried to pick up her glass of champagne but her hand was shaking and she put it back down on the small table between them. "I won't let him do it," she said. "I don't want Kim to ever know that she was conceived because I was raped."

"But if it comes out..." Linc ran his hand across his chin. "If you tell her the truth, Eden, about your being her mother, she's going to be curious about who her real father is. Have you thought about that?"

"Yes," she said quietly. "I'm going to tell her that her father was a college student and that I was still in high school and too young to be married."

"I see." He refilled her glass.

"Please try to understand why I have to tell her, why this is so important to me. I'm her mother, Linc. I want her to know how much I love her. I want to make up to her for all the years I haven't been there for her."

"I know that you think you're right, Eden, but—"

"I'd never do anything to hurt her, Linc. Or you. I don't want to hurt you." She touched his hand. "She loves you so much. You're her father. Nothing will ever change that."

Her face was so intent, her green eyes so anxious in their appeal for his understanding. He loved her and he knew that no matter what happened, that would not change. Somehow, when it was all said and done, they would come through this.

He took a small blue velvet box out of his shirt pocket. "This is for you," he said.

Eden looked at him in surprise. Her heart skipped six beats and her hands began to shake. She opened the lid and saw a pear-shaped diamond nestled beside a plain gold wedding band.

"I want to marry you," Linc said.

She couldn't get her breath. Her whole life, everything, converged on this one moment in time. "I...I don't know what to say," she whispered.

"Say yes."

She ran her fingertips over the rings. "I have to know," she said in an unsteady voice. "I have to know if you're doing this because of Kim. Because it will be better for her if we're married."

"No," he said. "It's because of you, Eden. Because I love you and I can't imagine living the rest of my life without you."

He took her left hand and slid the pear-shaped diamond onto her finger. "I love you, Eden," he said. "Say that you'll marry me."

The diamond twinkled as bright as the tears that formed and fell. She loved him, and yes, she knew that he loved her.

He stood and drew her up into his arms.

"I love you." She pressed her cheek to his. "Oh, I love you so much."

"Say that you'll marry me, Eden."

She raised her face for his kiss. "I'll marry you," she said against his lips.

They watched the moon come up over the water and in a little while they went down below and fixed sandwiches and a salad. And when they had finished eating they went back up to the deck.

They could see the lights from the distant shore and it was good to be like this, away from all the busyness of life, alone here on the quiet sea under a canopy of stars. Linc put pillows down on the deck and they lay together and looked up at the night sky.

They were alone on the sea, free for this space of time from the bonds of civilization. The boat rocked gently beneath them, the offshore breeze caressed their skin. They stroked each other, and kissed, and when it became too much, their bodies joined in a quiet celebration of life and of love.

In that final moment when it seemed to Eden that all of the stars in the heavens had converged into one great shining light, she held him and kissed him and said, "I love you, Linc. Always and forever, Linc."

When they were in the car he said, "Kim's going to be happy about the engagement. But let's not tell her everything at once. It's enough now for her to know that we're going to be married. Let's wait for a little while before we tell her that you're her mother."

The slightest of frowns drew Eden's brows together, but she nodded and said, "All right, Linc. We'll let her get used to the idea that we're going to be married first."

Kim was still awake, watching the end of a Western on the VCR when they came in, but Phoebe Rose was sound asleep in one of the recliners, head back, snoring gently.

"Hi." Kim reached for the remote control and snapped off the VCR. "Have a good time? Where'd you go?"

"To Bonita." Linc grinned down at Phoebe Rose. "We'd better wake her."

"Why not let her sleep in my room tonight?" Kim eased her leg off the sofa.

"All right." He looked at Eden and then back to Kim. "Eden and I have something to tell you," he said.

"What?" She frowned, and to Eden she said, "You're going back to Michigan, aren't you?"

"No, Kim, I'm not going back."

"Then what?" She looked at Linc. Two bright spots of color rose in her cheeks and she began to smile. "What is it?" she cried. "Tell me."

"Why don't we wake Phoebe Rose first." Eden touched the other woman's shoulder and gently shook her.

Phoebe Rose opened her eyes.

"Dad and Eden have something to tell us," Kim said excitedly.

"Then I reckon I'm wide-awake."

Kim turned an expectant gaze on her father, then on Eden. "What is it?" she asked.

He reached for Eden's hand. "I asked Eden to marry me tonight."

"And she said yes?" With a delighted cry Kim threw her arms around her father, then around Eden. "Oh, Eden," she said. "I hoped and hoped this would happen. I'm so glad. Can I be in the wedding?"

"Who else would I want to be my maid of honor?"

"Your maid of honor! Really? Thank you, oh, thank you."

"My!" Phoebe Rose sat up. "My, oh my. You and Dr. Linc. Now isn't that fine. Isn't that just fine." She got up and came over to shake Linc's hand and to embrace Eden. "When's the wedding going to be?"

"Whenever Kim's up to walking down the aisle with me." Eden put an arm around Kim's shoulders. "October's a nice month," she said.

"Hurricane season." Phoebe Rose shook her head. "But I reckon you won't let a hurricane stop you even if one does decide to hit."

Linc put one arm around Eden and the other around Kim. "Nothing's going to stop our wedding," he said.

"What are you going to wear?" Kim asked Eden. "What about pink? You look beautiful in pink."

"It'll depend on what we can find. I'd like our dresses to be similar..." Mother and daughter dresses, she almost said. But didn't.

They chatted and planned and when Kim got tired, Linc carried her up the stairs, and Phoebe Rose said she'd help Kim to bed.

When Linc walked Eden to the door of her room he put his arm around her. "Let's make it early in October," he said.

"The sooner the better." Eden kissed his cheek.

"Waiting isn't going to be easy." He hesitated. "I'd like you to stay here, Eden, instead of going back to the house with Phoebe Rose. It would mean a lot to Kim if you did."

"All right, Linc." She kissed him again, this time on the mouth. "Good night," she said when she stepped away from him. "Good night, darling."

* * *

They decided that on the following Saturday the three of them would go sailing. Kim hadn't been on the boat since her accident and she was longing to go.

"We'll tell her Saturday," Eden said. "If that's all right with you."

"If that's what you want. If you're sure."

"I'm sure," she said.

He worried about it all that week, for in spite of the fact that Kim loved Eden and that she was pleased about the coming marriage, he was terrified of how she would react when she learned that Eden was her mother. What would she say to Eden? Eden who had given her up on the day she was born.

And what about Kim's reaction to him? How would she feel when she found out that he and Carolyn had lied to her?

"Maybe we should wait until after the wedding to tell her," he said.

But Eden shook her head. "I'm scared, too, Linc," she said, "but it's going to be all right. I know it's going to be all right."

Early on Saturday morning the hospital called to say that a patient of his, a Mrs. Lonnigan, had been admitted and that she was in serious condition. Linc dressed hurriedly, debated whether to awaken Eden or to leave a note for her, and decided he'd better awaken her.

"What is it?" she asked when she opened her door.

"I have to go to the hospital. I'll get home as soon as I can. Go back to sleep."

But Eden didn't go back to sleep. Instead she lay awake thinking how it would be today when she told Kim that she was her mother.

For the first time since she had made the decision to tell Kim the truth a shadow of doubt crept over her. How would Kim react when she learned the truth? Would she be angry? Would she be able to understand how very young and frightened Eden had been when she'd given her up?

At seven she went downstairs and made a pot of coffee. As soon as she heard Kim beginning to move around she fixed two glasses of fresh orange juice and took them upstairs.

Kim was propped up in bed reading.

"Your dad had to go to the hospital," Eden said. "We'll leave for the boat as soon as he comes back. Why don't I fix a couple of trays and we'll have breakfast up here?"

"That'd be great, Eden. We can talk about the wedding."

"You bet." Eden kissed Kim on her forehead. "What are you reading?"

"A book of poetry that belonged to my mother. I haven't read any poetry in a long time and I'd forgotten how much I like it." She put the book down. "Can we have French toast?"

"With very crisp bacon?"

"*Burn* it," Kim said.

Eden hummed to herself while she prepared breakfast. It's going to be a good day, she told herself. It's going to be all right when I tell her.

Kim was still reading when Eden came in. She looked up. There were tears on her cheeks.

"Darling," Eden said. "What is it?"

"I haven't looked at this book of mother's since she died."

Eden put the trays down and came to sit on the edge of the bed beside Kim. She tried to keep her face impassive, her smile gentle. Carolyn wasn't your mother, she wanted to say. I am. And suddenly she knew that she was going to tell her. Now. She wasn't going to wait for this afternoon. I'll let her read the damn poem, she thought, and when she's finished I'll tell her. I'll tell her the truth.

"She'd marked a poem of Christina Rossetti's. She wrote in the margin, Eden. Look."

And Eden read, "This is for you, my darling Kim."

Her heart began a hard unsteady beat.

Kim wiped her eyes and began to read.

"When I am dead, my dearest,
Sing no sad songs for me;
Plant thou no roses at my head,
Nor shady cypress tree:
Be the green grass above me
With showers and dewdrops wet;
And if thou wilt, remember,
And if thou wilt, forget."

She loved me, Eden." Kim clutched the book to her breast. "Mama loved me. Sometimes when she was sick, when she'd close herself away in her room, I used to think that she didn't. But she did, Eden. Now I know that she did."

Something twisted inside Eden, a feeling she had never had before, a feeling that made her heart constrict with pain. For she knew now that Carolyn had, in every sense of the word, been Kim's mother. In spite of her weaknesses, her nerves and her neuroses, she had loved and cared for Kim as she would have for a child she had borne.

She had been a part of Kim's life for fifteen years, and Kim had loved her. How could she diminish the memory of that love?

Dear God, how could she have been so unaware of Kim's need to know that Carolyn had loved her? How could she take that away from Kim?

Once before, she had been called upon to make a sacrifice for the sake of her child. She had done it then, she could do it now because she loved Kim far more than she had ever realized she could love. And she knew that she could not, that she would not, do anything to hurt her.

And though she wept inside, she smiled at Kim. She said, "Of course your mother loved you, Kimmy."

And when Kim had wiped away her tears and smiled again, Eden made herself eat a little of the French toast and some of the very crisp, almost burned bacon.

Eden was in the garden alone when Linc came home late that morning.

"I got away as soon as I could," he said. "I'll just wash up and change..." He saw her tears. "What is it?" he asked. "Eden, what is it?"

"I can't do it," she whispered. "I can't tell her."

Linc knelt on the grass beside her.

"I love her so much."

"I know, Eden. I know, my love."

"This morning when I took her her breakfast tray she was reading a book of poetry. It had been Carolyn's book, Linc. She'd marked a poem for Kim. She'd written in the margin, 'This is for you, my darling Kim.' It was Rossetti's poem, 'When I am dead, my dearest...'"

Eden couldn't go on. She put her hands over her face and began to weep.

Linc drew her into his arms.

"It was Carolyn who was there for Kim, Linc," she wept against his shoulder. "It wasn't me. It was never me. Kim loved her and I can't . . . I can't take that away from her.''

He smoothed the hair back from her face. ''Are you sure, Eden?''

She looked up at him. ''Yes,'' she said. ''And it's all right, Linc. I have Kim and I have you. That's so much more than I ever dreamed or hoped for.''

He cupped her face between his hands. He gently kissed her, and knew that he had never loved her as much as he did at that moment.

The wedding took place in the garden on the first day of October. The sky was a cloudless blue, the air was soft.

Roses lined the path leading to the bowered altar where the minister waited.

Kim came down the path first. Her leg was strong and straight; she looked like an angel in the long pink gown that was just a shade darker than Eden's.

Eden carried pink roses. Baby's breath and forget-me-nots were woven in her hair.

At the altar she joined hands with Linc, and smiled up at him when the minister said the words that bound them together as man and wife.

''I'm so happy,'' Kim whispered to Eden when the ceremony ended. ''I feel as though we're really related now. As though you really are my mother.''

''I am,'' Eden said with a smile. ''I'm your number-two mother and I love you.''

Linc squeezed her hand. He knew what the sacrifice had cost Eden. She never spoke of it, but he knew.

And he loved her, his wife, his love, his Eden.

Epilogue

Seven years had sped by. There were touches of silver in Linc's hair now, but if anything he was more handsome than ever.

"You're going to be the best-looking grandfather in the state of Florida," Eden told him that morning when they were having breakfast. She shook her head. "It's almost impossible to believe that Kim is married, let alone that she's having a baby."

"Clay's fault," Linc growled.

"Not entirely." Eden passed him another slice of toast. "Kim had her eye on him for years. Frankly I don't think Clay had a chance."

"At least he had the decency to let her grow up before he married her."

Eden smiled. Now and then Linc complained about Clay's having robbed the cradle by marrying Kim, but she knew that he liked Clay and that he was pleased that the younger couple's marriage was a happy one.

Two years ago he and Clay had opened offices with two other doctors in a new medical center near Ft. Myers. Though their fields of expertise were different, they got along well and often consulted with each other on special cases.

In another two weeks Kim would have her baby. She hadn't had amniocentesis because, she said, "I want to be surprised. Clay wants a boy but I'm hoping for a girl."

"You'll both be delighted," Eden told her. "No matter what you have."

"I know we will. We—" Kim's expression changed. "She's moving, Eden. Quick, give me your hand. Can you feel her?"

"She's going to be a star halfback," Eden said with a laugh. "Oh, just feel that. She's kicking up a storm."

These past eight and a half months had been almost as exciting for Eden as they had been for Kim. Kim had shared generously in the joy of her pregnancy. They had shopped together for maternity clothes and baby clothes. Eden had helped her through the first months of morning queasiness and she'd been as excited as Kim the first time the baby moved.

The baby kicked again and Kim covered Eden's hand with her own. "I'm so sorry you never had a baby," she said. "You'd have made a wonderful mother, Eden. I was hoping that after you and Dad got married that you might."

"So was I, Kim, but we couldn't. I couldn't."

She had wanted to. More than anything in the world she'd wanted to have Linc's baby.

"I won't let you risk it," he'd said.

But because she had insisted, he'd arranged for her to consult with a doctor in Miami. "I doubt you could get pregnant," the specialist had said. "But if you did it would be dangerous for both you and the baby. I strongly advise against it."

Kim was the only child she was ever to have, and though she would have liked things to have been different, Eden was grateful for all that she had. She loved Linc, and Kim was her daughter in every sense of the word.

There had been times during the past seven years when she had questioned her decision not to tell Kim the truth. It was especially hard now when her grandchild was due. But she had made a decision and she would stick to it. Kim would never know that she was her mother.

Nor would she ever know that Dave Fenwell was her father. Two years ago Dave had been killed in a prison riot. The fear that she'd always had that someday he might make trouble, faded.

So now she patted Kim's stomach and they made jokes about how little what's-her-name would be a star half-back for the University of Miami.

"I wish you'd give the poor little thing a name," Eden said.

"I'll name her when she's born," Kim answered with a smile.

That's what Eden had said so long ago. "I'll know when I look at her," she'd told Aunt Jo. "And even though I know it won't ever be her name, it will always be my special name for her."

But there hadn't been time. She'd held Kim only for a moment before Linc had taken her away. But later, the first time she had seen Kim, she had known that the name he and Carolyn had chosen was perfect.

She was Kim, always and forever Kim. Her daughter.

On a Sunday morning, a week before Kim was due to deliver, she and Linc went to church. Clay had gone to Miami as a consultant on a particularly difficult case and Kim had been spending the weekend with Linc and Eden. On Sunday morning, Eden, who had been getting over a cold, said, "You two go to church and stay out for brunch. I'm saving my strength for when the baby comes."

So Linc and a very pregnant Kim had gone to church and then to brunch together.

"Eden's taken such good care of me all through this," Kim said when she eased herself into a chair at the restaurant. "She's done as much for me as my real mother would have done, Dad. I love her so much."

"And she loves you," he said.

"I haven't told her yet because I want it to be a surprise, but if the baby's a girl I'm going to name her Eden."

"That's nice, sweetheart. Eden will be awfully pleased."

"I wanted to do something special for her. I told her the other day that I wish she'd had children. She'd have made a wonderful mother."

"Yes," he said quietly. "She would have."

"Do you remember Emily Gebhart? I went through high school with her."

"Yes, I remember her."

"She was an adopted child, you know. I used to think that was the worst thing anybody could be, but I don't anymore, since I've been pregnant, I mean. It must be terrible to have to give your baby away, for whatever reason. It must be just terrible."

"It is," he said. "It's terrible." He reached across the table and took Kim's hand. "I have something to tell you," he said. "I should have told you a long time ago."

The call came in the middle of the night.

"It's Clay," Eden said before Linc could answer. She switched the light on and sat up.

"Hello?" Linc said. "Clay?"

Eden grasped his hand.

Linc listened and nodded. "We're on our way." He tightened his grip on Eden's hand. "Tell her we're coming."

When he put the phone down, Eden was already pulling on a pair of jeans. "Is she all right?" she asked. "Is anything wrong?"

"No." Linc reached for his pants. "The pains are still twenty minutes apart." He tried to sound reassuring but his hands were damp with fear. "It's going to be fine," he said, and realized he was trying to put his left shoe on his right foot.

They made the ten-minute ride to the hospital in five, and when they went in, they found Clay pacing up and down in front of Kim's room.

"McCluskey's with her," he said. "I'm afraid it's going to be a long night." He ran a distracted hand through his hair. "This is awful," he said. "I'll never go through this again."

"*You'll* never go through it," Linc muttered. "That's my daughter in there."

Eden took each of their arms. "Let's go sit down and have a cup of coffee," she said. "McCluskey will know where to find us."

She bought the coffee from a machine at the end of the corridor. The three of them took a couple of sips and went back to wait in front of Kim's door.

At last, McCluskey came out. "She's doing fine," he said so cheerfully that Eden wanted to throttle him. He clapped Clay on the back. "You'll be coaching her so try not to fall apart."

Clay swore under his breath.

"She wants you in the delivery room, too, Eden. I'll let you know when it's time to suit up."

Eden reached for Linc's hand. "I didn't know I'd be doing that," she said. "I've never..." She swallowed hard. "But I'm glad she wants me with her."

As Clay had predicted, it was a long night. Almost five hours went by before one of the nurses said, "She's ready to go into the delivery room."

Eden kissed Kim's cheek. "It won't be long now," she said. She put her arms around Linc. "It's going to be fine," she told him, and prayed that it would be.

It wasn't an easy delivery, but Kim was brave and so was Clay. He held her hand, he helped her to breathe. "Easy does it, sweetheart," he said. "Hang on, Kimbo. Hang on tight, darling."

"Am I doing okay?" she asked. "I don't want to make a fuss."

But in a little while, the pains came hard, so hard that she cried out. She reached for Eden's hand, eyes closed, holding tight. "Don't let go," she cried. "Don't let go, Mother."

And when she opened her eyes she said, "I know. Dad told me. And I'm glad, I'm so glad. That's why I wanted you here." She reached up and wiped Eden's tears away with her fingertips. "Don't cry, Mama," she said. "Don't cry."

At five minutes after six that morning, Eden Rose Contney was born. She weighed seven and one quarter pounds, she was eighteen inches long and her head was covered with blond fuzz.

"Just like us," Kim said when she gave Eden the baby to hold.

Linc put his arm around his wife's shoulders as she looked down at their grandchild. He touched the baby's small hand and she curled her fist around his finger.

"I love you," he said to Eden, and to Kim and to the new little Eden. "I love you."

* * * * *

Silhouette Special Edition

proudly presents
the long-awaited "prequel" volume of

LOVE AND GLORY
★ ★

by
LINDSAY McKENNA
Dawn of Valor

In the summer of '89, Silhouette Special Edition premiered three novels celebrating America's men and women in uniform: LOVE AND GLORY, by bestselling author Lindsay McKenna. Featured were the proud Trayherns, a military family as bold and patriotic as the American flag—three siblings valiantly battling the threat of dishonor, determined to triumph . . . in love and glory.

Now, discover the roots of the Trayhern brand of courage, as parents Chase and Rachel relive their earliest heartstopping experiences of survival and indomitable love, in

Dawn of Valor, Silhouette Special Edition #649

This month, experience the thrill of LOVE AND GLORY—from the very beginning!

Silhouette Books®

DV-1A

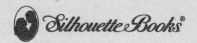

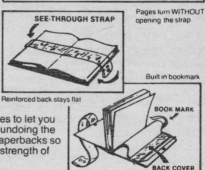

WRITTEN IN THE STARS

MAN FROM THE NORTH COUNTRY
by Laurie Paige

What does Cupid have planned for
the Aquarius man? Find out in February in
MAN FROM THE NORTH COUNTRY by
Laurie Paige—the second book in our
WRITTEN IN THE STARS series!

Brittney Chapel tried explaining the sensible
side of marriage to confirmed bachelor
Daniel Montclair, but the gorgeous grizzly bear
of a man from the north country wouldn't
respond to reason. What was a woman to do
with an unruly Aquarian? Tame him!

Spend the most romantic month of the year with
MAN FROM THE NORTH COUNTRY by
Laurie Paige in February... only from
Silhouette Romance.

FEBSTAR